HARRY HARRISON

PLANET OF NO RETURN

A TOM DOHERTY ASSOCIATES BOOK

PLANET OF NO RETURN

Copyright © 1982 by Harry Harrison

First Tor printing: January 1982

A TOR Book

Published by Tom Doherty Associates, Inc.
49 West 24 Street
New York, N.Y. 10010

Cover art by Michael Whelan

Interior Illustration by Rick DeMarco

ISBN: 0-812-53981-8
CAN. ED.: 0-812-53982-6

Printed in the United States of America

0 9 8 7 6 5 4 3 2 1

PLANET
OF
NO
RETURN

TABLE OF CONTENTS

ONE

One Man Alone

As the small spacecraft plunged into the first thin traces of the planet's atmosphere it began to glow and burn like a falling meteor. Within seconds the glow spread, quickly changing from red to white as the frictional heat increased. Although the alloy of the metal skin was unbelievably strong it had never been intended to resist temperatures as high as these. Sheets of flame radiated from the nose cone as the metal was torn away, incinerated. Then, just when it appeared that the entire ship would be engulfed in fire and destroyed, the even brighter flames of braking jets lanced through the burning gas. If the craft had been falling out of control it would surely have been destroyed. But the pilot knew what he was doing, had waited until the last possible moment before destruction before firing his engines. To slow the ship's fall just enough to keep the temperature from rising any higher.

Down through the thick clouds it dropped, down towards the grass covered plain that hurtled ever closer with alarming speed. When it appeared that a fatal crash was inevitable the rockets fired again, hammering at the ship with multiple G decelleration. Still falling rapidly, despite the roaring jets, the ship struck the ground with a resounding crash, depressing the landing shock absorbers to their limit.

As the clouds of steam and dust blew away, a small metal hatch at the apex of the bow ground open and an optic head slowly emerged. It began rotating in a slow circle, scanning the vast sea of grass, the distant trees, the seemingly empty landscape. A herd of animals moved in the distance, bounding away in panic and quickly vanishing from sight. The optic head moved on—finally coming to rest on the nearby ruins of the shattered war machines: a vast area of destruction in the cratered plain.

It was a scene of disaster. Hundreds, perhaps thousands, of the crumpled and gigantic weapons of war were scattered over the battlefield. All of them punctured, bent, torn by immense forces. It was a graveyard of destruction that stretched away almost to the horizon. The optic head scanned back and forth over the rusted hulks, stopped, then drew back into the ship and its cover plate snapped shut. Long minutes passed before the silence was broken by the squeal of metal on metal as the airlock ground slowly open.

More time passed before the man emerged slowly from the opening. His motions were cautious, the muzzle of the ion rifle he held was questing out before him like a hungry animal. He wore heavy space armor with a sealed helmet that used a TV unit for vision. Slowly, without taking his attention from the landscape or his finger from the trigger, the man lowered his free hand and touched the radio button on his wrist.

"I'm continuing my report from outside the ship now. I'm going slow until I get my breath back. My bones ache. I made the landing in free fall and held it at that for just as long as I could. It was a fast landing but I took at least 15 G's on touchdown. If I was detected on the way down there is no evidence of it yet. I'm going to keep talking as I go. This broadcast is being recorded on my deepspacer up above me in planetary orbit. So no matter what happens to me there is going to be a record kept. I'm not going to do an incompetent job like Marcill."

He didn't regret saying it, putting his feelings about the dead man in the record. If Marcill had taken any precautions at all he might still be alive. But precautions or no the fool should have found a way to leave some message. But there was nothing, absolutely nothing to indicate what had happened, not a single word that might have helped him now. Hartig snorted through his nostrils at the thought. Landing on a new planet was a danger every time, no matter how peaceful it looked. And this one, Selm-II, was certainly no different. Far from peaceful looking. It had been Marcill's first assignment. And his last. The man had reported in from planetary orbit and had recorded his proposed landing position on the surface. And nothing else after that. A fool. He had never been heard from again. That was when the decision had been made to call a specialist in. This was Hartig's seventeenth planet contact. He intended to use all of his experience to see to it that it wasn't his last as well.

"I can see why Marcill picked this spot. There's nothing but grass, empty plain stretching out in all directions. But right here, next to this landing site, there has been a battle—and not too long ago either. The remains of the fighting are just in front of me. There appear to be war machines of various kinds, pretty impressive things at one time, but all of them blasted apart and rusting now. I'm going to take a closer look at them."

Hartig sealed the lock and started warily towards the littered battlefield, reporting as he went. "These machines are big, the nearest one to me must be at least fifty yards long. It has tractor treads and is mounted with a single turret with a large gun. That's destroyed now. No identification visible from this distance. I'm going to take a closer look at it. But I can tell you frankly that I don't like this. There were no cities visible from space, no broadcasts or transmissions on any of the communication bands. Yet here is this battlefield and these wrecks. And they're not toys. These things are the products of a very advanced technology. Nor are they any kind of illusion. This thing is solid metal—and it has been blown open by something even solider. Still no insignia or identification anywhere on it that I can see. I'm going to take a look inside. There are no hatches visible from where I'm standing, but there is a hole blown in the side big enough to drive a truck through. I'm going through it now. There may be documents inside, certainly ought to be labels of some kind on the controls . . ."

Hartig stopped, frozen, one gloved hand clutching

the jagged rim of metal around the opening. Had he heard something? With careful motions he raised the gain on his external microphone. But all he could hear now was the wind sighing through the metal skeletons. Nothing else. He listened for awhile, then shrugged and turned to climb through the gaping wound into the machine.

With startling suddenness a distant mechanical clanking echoed from the metal corpses of the battlefield. Hartig turned and dropped, his gun pointing and ready.

"There's something out there, moving. Can't see it yet—but I can hear it clearly enough. I've switched the external mike to this circuit so the sound will be recorded too. It's getting louder, wheels, treads maybe, squeaking and clanking. A machine . . . *there!*"

With a crash of metal against metal the thing appeared from among the ruined machines. It was smaller than most of the others, no more than five yards long, and hurtled along with frightening speed. Smoothly black and sinister. Hartig raised his gun, then eased his finger from the trigger when he saw that it was turning away from him. Twisting about and accelerating at the same time.

"It's heading towards my landing ship! It may have detected it when I sat down. Found it by radiation, radar, something. I'm using my remote unit to set all the defenses aboard. As soon as that thing gets within range it will be blasted . . . there!"

Explosion after explosion sounded as the rapid-fire guns aboard the lifeship poured out their deadly fire. The ground shook and fragments of rock and

dirt where hurled into the air. The guns stopped—
and in an instant began firing again as the machine
emerged from the dust. Apparently unharmed.

"That thing is fast and tough, but the primaries
will get it . . ."

An even greater explosion shook the ground,
clanging through the metal walls around him; a
shower of red dust floated down. Hartig stared out,
frozen, then began talking again in a toneless voice.

"That was my ship going up. It took just a single
shot from that damned thing. Our guns couldn't
touch it. Now it's turning in this direction. It must
be tracking my radio signal, heat radiation, something. No point in turning the radio off now. It's
coming this way—straight at me. I'm shooting now
but it doesn't seem to affect it. I can't see any ports or
windows facing this way. The crew must see by TV
relay. I'm trying to shoot out some protrusions on
the thing's front. They may be pickups. Instrumen-
tation of some kind. Doesn't seem to slow it down—"

The sound of the explosion terminated abruptly
as the radio broadcast ended. In orbit, high above,
the control center in the deep spacer began to search
automatically for the radio signal, but without any
success. Then it tried all of the other broadcast
channels. There was nothing. With mechanical
tenacity it started over once again and searched
with maximum gain, but detected nothing other
than atmospherics. After one hour it repeated the
search, and every hour after that for the next
twenty-four. When this part of the program had
been completed it turned on the FTL radio as it had
been instructed and sent out the broadcast it had

recorded from the man on the ground. When this
had been accomplished it would down the power on
all of its circuits to minimum maintenance, then
wait with infinite patience for its next command.

TWO

The Smell of Death

"What is it? What's wrong?" Lea asked. Her shoulder had felt the sudden tensing of Brion's body where it touched him. They were lying back on the deep lounge, completely relaxed, gazing out of the viewing port at the star-filled darkness of interstellar space. His great arm was about her thin body and she was very aware of its sudden rigidity.

"Nothing is wrong, nothing at all. Will you look at those colors . . ."

"Listen, you darling big slab of muscle, you may be the best weightlifter in the galaxy—but you are also the worst liar. Something has happened. Something I don't know about."

Brion hesitated a moment, then nodded. "There's someone close by, someone who hasn't been here before. Someone bringing trouble."

"I believe in your empathetic abilities, I've seen them at work. So I know that you can sense other peoples emotions. But we're in deep space, moving between two suns light years apart—so how can there be anyone new aboard this ship . . ." She stopped and looked suddenly out at the stars. "A drop sphere, of course. This must be a rendezvous, not just a normal orientation. Is there another FTL ship out there? With someone transfering from it in a drop sphere?"

"Not coming—already arrived. He's on board now. And he's coming this way, towards us. I don't like anything about this. I don't like the man—or the message that he is bringing."

With a single flowing motion Brion was on his feet, facing about, fists clenched. Although he was well over six feet tall and weighed nearly three-hundred pounds, he moved like a cat. Lea looked up at the solid mass of him towering over her and could almost feel the tension herself.

"You can't be sure," she said quietly. "Undoubtedly you are right about someone coming aboard. But it doesn't necessarily mean that it has anything to do with us . . ."

"One man dead, two men perhaps. And this one who is coming, he smells of death himself. He's here now."

Lea gasped as she heard the lounge door sliding open behind her. She looked over her shoulder fearfully, staring at the opening, not knowing what to expect. There was the shuffle of a soft footstep, then a thud. Shuffle, thud. Closer and louder. Then a man appeared in the open doorway, hesitated there as he looked about, blinking as though he had trouble seeing.

It took a decided effort for Lea to conceal her

instant feeling of repulsion; she had to force herself not to look away. The man's single eye moved slowly past her to fix on Brion. Then he started forward again, his twisted foot dragging, the crutch coming down heavily with each step. Whatever force had injured his legs must have also torn away the right side of his face. It was bright pink where a new growth of skin; a patch covered the empty eye socket. His right arm was also missing, but an arm bud had been grafted to his clavicle and within a year he would have a complete, new arm. But right now it was only partly grown, a baby's arm only about a foot long that dangled helplessly from his shoulder. He limped close, slight and twisted, to stand before Brion's hulking form.

"I'm Carver," he said, his name a frightful parody of his condition. "I'm here to see you, Brandd."

"I know." The tension drained from Brion's body as suddenly as it had appeared. "Sit down and rest."

Lea could not stop herself from moving aside as Carver dropped, sighing, onto the lounge beside her. She could hear his heavy breathing, see the perspiration standing out on his skin as he fumbled a capsule from his pocket and put it into his mouth. He looked sideways at her and nodded. "Doctor Lea Morees," he said. "They want you too."

"Culrel?" Brion asked. Carver nodded.

"The Cultural Relationships Foundation. I understand you have worked with us before?"

"We did. It was an emergency . . ."

"It's always an emergency. Something very important has come up. I was sent to see you."

"Why us? We've just come from a hell-hole of a planet named Dis. Lea has been ill. We were promised some more time before we would be contacted. We agreed to work for your people again, but not right now . . .''

"I told you—it's always an emergency." Carver's voice was hoarse and he pressed his good hand between his knees to stop the trembling. It was pain or fatigue—or both—and he was not giving in to it. "I've just come from another one of these emergencies, as you can see, or I would be going myself. If it makes you feel any better I know what happened to you both on Dis so I offered to take care of this one myself. They laughed at me. I don't think it was very funny. Are you both ready now?" He turned to face Brion as he said it.

"You can't force Lea to go, not now. I'll take care of it myself." Carver shook his head.

"You're to go as a team, the orders were specific about that. Shared talents, a synergistic union . . .''

"I'm going with Brion," Dea said. I'm feeling much better. By the time we get wherever we're going I'll be back to normal."

"That's very pleasing to hear. As you know we are a fully voluntary organization." He ignored Brion's snort of derision as he struggled a flat plastic box from the pocket of his tunic. "As I am sure you are aware, almost all of our assignments deal only with cultures that are in trouble, societies on planets that have been cut off from the mainstream of human contact for thousands of years. We don't go near newly rediscovered planets—that's the job of Planetary Survey. They go in first, then turn their records over to us. They're a rough outfit, I did four years with Plansurv before I transferred to Culrel."

He smiled grimly. "I thought this new job would be easier. Plansurv has a problem and they have asked us for help. In cases like this we always say yes. Are you ready to look at these records now?"

"I'll get a viewer from our cabin," Brion said.

Carver nodded wearily, too tired to speak.

"Would you like me to order you something?" Lea asked as Brion went out of the lounge.

"Yes, thank you, a drink of some kind. I'll wash down a pill with it—feel better in a few minutes. But no alcohol, I can't take any of that yet."

She felt his eyes on her as she phoned passenger control and gave her order to the computer. When she had finished the call she put back the phone and turned sharply to face him.

"Well—do you like what you see?"

"Sorry. I didn't mean to stare. But I read your history in the records. I never met anyone from Earth before."

"What did you expect—two heads?"

"I said that I was sorry. Before I left my home world and went into space I really believed that the whole story of Earth was just another religious myth."

"Well, now you can see for yourself that we are real undernourished flesh and blood. Underfed citizens of an overcrowded and worn out planet. Probably just what we deserve, I imagine you would say."

"No. I might have at one time. No more. I'm sure that the Earth Empire was guilty of a number of excesses, just the sort of thing we read about in our school books. No one's in doubt about that. But all of that's just history now, ancient history thousands of years in the past. What is of much greater impor-

tance to me is the fate of all the planets that were cut off after the Breakdown. It wasn't until I saw for myself what had happened to some of them that I knew what an unyielding and harsh universe it could be. Mankind basically belongs only on Earth. You may feel personally inferior because the over-crowding and limited resources have caused an overall reduction in your size. But you belong on Earth—and are a product of Earth. A number of us may appear larger or stronger than you—but this is because we have been forced to adapt to some cruel and violent worlds. I've become used to that—I even accept it as the norm. It wasn't until I saw you that I realized that the home of mankind was still a reality." He smiled a crooked grin.

"Please don't think me foolish for saying this," he said, "but I experienced a sensation of both pleasure—and relief—when I met you. Like a child discovering his long-lost parents. I'm afraid I'm not saying this very well. It's like coming home after a long voyage. I have seen the way mankind has adapted to a score of planets. Meeting you is, in a funny way a reassuring bit of knowledge. Our home is still there. I am very happy to meet you."

"I believe you, Carver." She smiled. "And I'm forced to admit that I'm beginning to like you too. Though I have to admit that you are not too good to look at."

He laughed and leaned back, sipping at the cold drink that had been delivered automatically to the table at his side. "Give me a year and you'll never recognize me."

"I am sure that will be true. I'm a biologist, an exobiologist, so I know in theory what can be done with restoration growth, I'm sure that you will be as good as new after some time. But that's just theory—I've never seen it in practice before. We're not rich on Earth, so few of us can afford massive reconstruction like yours."

"This is one of the few benefits of working for Culrel. They put you back together again no matter how badly you get butchered. I'm going to have a new eye behind this patch in a few months."

"How very nice. But speaking personally I would like to avoid all the benefits of this kind of reconstruction if you don't mind."

"Good luck in that—I don't blame you."

They both looked up as Brion returned with the viewer. He took the recording cartridge from Carver and slipped it into the mechanism. He and Lea bent close as the screen lit up. Carver collapsed back and listened to the recording while he sipped at his glass. He had heard it often before and he dozed a bit through the early material, but snapped awake as it approached the end. Hartig's recorded voice continued to speak, sounding calm and precise, although he faced certain extinction, still trying to the last to leave a record for those who would follow after him. Lea was horrified as the recording ended and the screen cleared; Brion's impassive face displayed no emotion as he turned to Carver.

"And Culrel wants us to go to this planet, Selm-II?" He asked. Carver nodded. "Why? This looks more like a job for the troops. Shouldn't they be sending something large and well armed that can take care of itself?"

"No. That's exactly what we don't want. Experience has proven that armed intrusion is never the

answer. War does not work. War kills. What we need is knowledge, information. We must know what is happening on this planet. We need skilled people like you two. Perhaps Dis was your first assignment, something that you were drafted into against your wishes. But you succeeded magnificently, doing what the specialists themselves said couldn't be done. We want you to put those talents to use here. I'll not deny that it could be terribly dangerous. But it must be done."

"I hadn't planned on living forever," Lea said, then leaned over to order some strong drinks. Her flippancy did not fool Brion.

"I'll go by myself," he said. "I can do this better alone."

"Oh no you can't, you great big brainless slab of muscle. You're not bright enough to be let out alone. I go with you or you don't go. Try to go by yourself and I will shoot you right here to save the expense of transporting you there just to be knocked off."

Brion smiled at this. "Your sympathy and understanding are most touching. I agree. Your logical arguments have convinced me that that it would be best if we went together."

"Good." She grabbed up the glass as soon as it appeared from the dispenser and drank deeply from it. "What's the next step, Carver?"

"A difficult one. We must convince the captain of this ship to change course and divert to Selm-II. An operational craft will be in orbit around the planet by now and will be waiting for us there."

"What's difficult about that?" Brion asked.

"I can see that you have never met the captain of a deep spacer before. They are all very firm minded.

And in absolute command while in flight. We can't force him to change course. We can only convince him."

"I'll convince him," Brion said, standing and looming large over them both. "We've taken on this assignment and no little spaceship driver is going to stand in our way."

THREE

A Desperate Plan

Captain M'Luta might be described in a number of ways. But never, by any reach of the imagination, could he be called a "little spaceship driver." He and Brion Brandd stood toe to toe, glaring at each other. They were both very large men, both solid and tall—if anything the Captain was a slight bit taller. He was as just as muscular as Brion—and equally pugnacious. They were very much alike in almost every way, with the slight difference that Brion's skin was a tanned bronze while the Captain's was a deep black.

"The answer is no," Captain M'Luta said, the coldness of his tone concealing his growing anger. "You may now leave my bridge."

"I don't think you understood me correctly, Captain. I was making a simple and informal request . . ."

"Good. Informal request denied."

"I haven't told you the reasons for this request yet . . ."

31

"Nor will you ever if I have my way. And I *will* have my way. I am the Captain of this ship. I have a crew, passengers, and a cargo to think of. As well as my schedule. These come first with me. At all times. This has already been disrupted by your people, for the contact and rendezvous to enable you to pick up a drop sphere. I did that because I was informed that it was an emergency. That emergency is now over. Will you leave or must I have you ejected?"

"Why don't you try."

Brion's voice was low, almost a whisper. But his fists were clenched, his muscles taut as he glared at the Captain. Who glared right back. Carver shuffled forward, pushing between them with some effort.

"This has gone far enough," he said. "Now I must intervene before the situation gets out of hand. Brandd, please join Dr. Morees. Now."

Brion took a deep breath and forced his muscles to relax. Carver was right—but he was still sorry that the Captain hadn't started a little trouble for him to finish. He spun on his heel and walked over to Lea, who was sitting on a bench against the bulkhead. As soon as the two men had been separated, Carver dug into his side pocket with his good hand and extracted a piece of paper, glanced at it briefly and put it away again.

"We had hoped for your voluntary cooperation, Captain M'Luta. But voluntary or not you will help us . . ."

"Officer of the watch," the Captain said into the microphone on his collar. "To the bridge at once with three ratings. Armed."

"Cancel that order at once," Carver said, angry himself now. "Get on the FTL communicator and call your base. Ask for Code Dp-L."

The Captain spun about sharply and loomed over the thin figure of the wounded man. "Where did you get that code?" he snapped the order. "Who are you?"

"No more questions if you please. Make that call and tell them that my name is Carver. Tell them that I am with you now."

The Captain did not answer, but they heard him cancelling his last command for armed assistance as he stamped across the bridge and into the communication compartment.

"What magic is that?" Brion asked as Carver dropped wearily onto the bench at his side.

"That's clout, not magic. The Captain's home world, Roodepoort, is one of those that owes a lot to the Cultural Relationships Foundation. The people on the planet may not know it—but the government does. They pay us a very large and completely voluntary contribution each year."

Brion nodded. "That means that Roodepoort is one of those worlds that Culrel aided in the past. We helped them out of trouble?"

"Perfectly correct. We can ask them for assistance, any amount—at any time. But it is the kind of debt that we collect only in an emergency. The director of their space agency has been informed of my presence here, and he has been told that his agency may expect a message about me. The director is a very busy executive and I don't think that she will enjoy being disturbed in this manner. Like it or not the Captain will cooperate."

They did not have very long to wait. The Captain stamped back onto the bridge, glowering like a thunderstorm, and stopped before Carver—who did not seem to be bothered at all by his threatening presence.

"Who are you, Carver? What makes you able to issue orders like this?"

"Since you have your orders—isn't that knowledge enough?"

"No. It is the law of space that I am the only one who can issue any commands on this ship. Now that law has been broken. My authority has been superceded. What if I chose not to obey these new instructions?"

"You could do that. But when you return to port you might find yourself in a small amount of trouble."

"Trouble?" The Captain smiled grimly. "I'll be on the beach. Finished."

"Then you put a high price on your curiosity. I wish to cause you no harm, Captain, please believe me. But it is desperately important that we make this diversion. I will tell you as much as I can. This is a Culrel operation. When you return home you can ask your superiors, the people who have issued you with your orders, what the name means. They are the ones who will decide how much you should know. All I can add is that this diversion is not a casual one. Lives have been lost already, and there will undoubtedly be more of them at stake in the future. Does that satisfy your curiosity?"

The Captain thudded his fist into the palm of his open hand with a sharp crack. "No," he said, "it does not. But it will have to do for the time being. We'll make the stop. But I don't want to see any of you aboard my ship. Ever again. I won't have this done to me a second time."

"We'll respect that wish, Captain. I'm sorry it had to be done this way at this time."

"Get out of here. You'll be informed of the time of the transfer."

"You haven't exactly made a friend there," Lea said as the door slammed solidly behind them. Carver shrugged, too weary to talk or care. "I'm going to my cabin," he said. "I'll join you again when we transfer."

All of the pleasure had gone out of the voyage for Lea and Brion. They reexamined the record and listened to Hartig's voice over and over again, so often that they had it memorized. Brion worked out in the ship's gymnasium, unaware of the fact that his weight lifting and general stamina gave the instructor a definite feeling of inferiority. Lea tried to rest and conserve her energy. She did not know what they would be facing on Selm-II, but the records had shown that it would be dangerous beyond belief. The waiting became unbearable and it was almost a relief to get the disembarkation notice. The Captain was not in sight when they made the transfer to the Culrel command ship.

"What happens next?" Brion asked, as the three of them emerged from the drop sphere inside the cavernous airlock of the ship.

"That is completely up to you," Carver said. "It's your assignment. You're the one in charge now."

"Where are we?"

"In orbit around Selm-II."

"I want to see it."

"There's an observation port in the lower lounge. This way. I'll have the Project Commander meet us there."

It was a large ship—and a busy one. They passed machine shops and storage bays, halted as robot-operated floater lifts drifted by carrying bulky loads. There was no one else in the observation lounge when they reached it. They stood on the transparent floor, looking down into space. The blue sphere of the planet lay below, half in shadow, illuminated by the fierce glow of the star, Selm, the sun to this solitary world. Brion stared at it with fierce concentration.

"From here it looks like any other planet. What brought about all the interest in it at this time?"

"It all began as a routine investigation—and that's really what it was at first. A normal computer search through some pre-Breakup records had discovered a list of shipments to various planets in the old Earth Empire. Most of these worlds were known, but of course there were a few that were new to us. Their coordinates were turned over to Plansurv for contact and identification. Since observation from space had revealed no cities or visible settlements, this planet was the last one to be surveyed. Nor was there any form of broadcasting activity in any of the communication bands."

"So there are no human beings here, or any signs of civilization—other than a few abandoned battlefields?"

"Yes—and that's what we found so intriguing. That military scrapheap that Marcill and Hartig landed near was the biggest one detected. But there are plenty more."

"Warfare—but no warriors. Where are all the people? Underground?"

"Perhaps. That is what you will have to find out after you have made a safe landing. The planet appears physically attractive enough. Those white polar caps you see are ice and snow. And there is a obviously a lot of ocean. There are islands and island chains, plus a single large continent just there. Half night and half day now. It is roughly bowl-shaped, and ringed about with mountain ranges. There are grass plains and hillside forest in the interior. Plenty of lakes, including that big one near the center where you can see the sunrise glinting on it, really an inland ocean. You'll get records of all this."

"What is the climate like?"

"Perfect. At least on the plains around the big lake. It gets a bit cooler in the mountains, but at the lower altitudes it is warm and comfortable."

"All right. The first thing we are going to need is transportation. What is available?"

"The Project Commander will take care of that for you. I suggest that you use one of the lifeships. They are compact landing vessels with plenty of power to spare, yet are still big enough to carry whatever equipment you may need. And they are well armed too. The techs will see to it that they stock the latest weaponry and defenses."

Brion raised his eyebrows at that. "The guns didn't seem to help Hartig very much."

"Then we can profit from his experience."

"Don't use *we* so freely," Lea said. "Unless you're planning to come along with us."

"Sorry. You can have whatever arms and weapons you might need. Both to take with you or have installed on the lifeship. The choice of equipment is yours."

"Let me have a list of what is available," Brion said.

"I'll take care of that," a voice said. They turned to see the thin, gray haired man who had entered silently while they were talking. He tapped a command into the communicator on his belt. "I'm Klart, your Project Commander. It is my responsibility to not only advise you but see to it that you get exactly what you want—and what you need. If you will look at the screen on the communicator over there you will see an index of the items we have in store."

The lists of available items were long and precise. Brion scrolled through them on the communicator, with Lea sitting beside him, touching the screen over the categories they were interested in. The

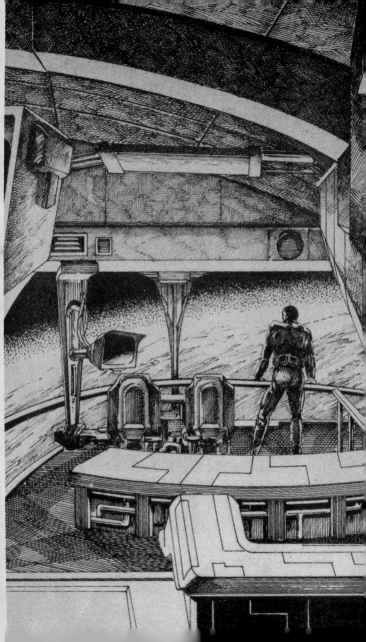

printouts began to pile up in the hopper beside them. Brion weighed them in his hands when they were done, then glanced at the planet below.

"I've reached a decision," he said. "And I hope Lea will agree. The lifeship will be armed and defended with all of the deadliest weapons that are available. We will also take every possible machine or device that might aid us on the planet. Then, when we are completely equipped, I am going down alone, without any machines or metallic devices of any kind. Bare handed if necessary. Lea, don't you agree that this will be the wisest course under the circumstances?"

Her speechless look of horror was his only answer.

FOUR

D-Day Minus One

"I'll draw up a list of recommendations at once," Klart said, entering a series of commands into his personal terminal. The calmness of his manner indicating that he could no longer be surprised by anything a field agent did or said. Lea did not share his attitude.

"Brion Brandd—anyone who says anything like that must be insane. Carver, see that he is locked up at once."

Carver nodded. "Lea is right. You can't just walk around unarmed in this sort of situation, on a deadly planet like this one. It would be suicide."

"Would it? Did all the machines and weapons help the two men who went before me? Marcill just vanished—but we now have a very good idea of what happened to him. And we know exactly what that killing machine did to Hartig. If you don't mind, I don't really want to go the way they went.

It's personal survival, not suicide that I'm thinking about. Before you make a decision I want you to consider two simple facts. Do you remember how Hartig died? The war machine came straight at him, targetted onto him by his radio or his weaponry. It detected him and destroyed him. Am I right?"

"So far," Lea said. "Is that fact number one?"

"It is. Hartig was detected and destroyed. Fact two are the animals. You will remember that Hartig described them just after he landed. In the distance, bounding away."

"And the relevance of these two pieces of information?" Carver asked.

"It's obvious," Lea told him. "The animals were alive and unbothered by the war machines. While Hartig was killed by them. So nature boy here is going to become an animal and prowl around on foot to sniff out the situation."

"That's insanity," Carver said. "I cannot permit it."

"You cannot stop it. Your responsibility ended when you got us here. I'm in command of the operation now. Lea stays with the lifeship in orbit. I land by myself."

"I take back what I said," Lea told them. "It's a sound plan. At least for a Winner of the Twenties." She saw Carver's blank gaze and laughed. "They couldn't have briefed you very well, Carver, if you didn't know that Brion is a world-wide hero. His home planet—which is one of the most uncomfortable in the galaxy—has an annual competition that is not only physical but mental. Twenty different events—everything from fencing to poetry composition, weight-lifting to chess. It must be the most grueling contest that ever existed, an exhausting demonstration of both physical and intellectual skills. You can ask Brion the details, but the result is an incredible sporting event that has only a single Winner at the end of the year's contests. Can you imagine a year-long athletic contest in which *everyone* on a planet participates? If you can absorb that—just think what the single victor of that contest must be like. If your imagination balks at that—why then just look at Brion here. He is one of those Winners. Whatever is causing the trouble on Selm-II—there is a very good chance that he will be able to take it on. And win."

Carver clumped over and dropped into a deep chair, the crutch falling by his side. "I believe you," he said. "Not that it makes any difference. As you said, what happens from now on is your responsibility. You're correct, I'm out of it. All I can do now is wish you good luck. Klart will see that you have everything that you might need."

"Here is a list of recommendations," Klart said, tearing a sheet from the printer and handing it over. Lea took it before Brion could.

"I'll be loafing about in the lifeship while you are on the surface, so taking care of the outfitting is my responsibility. You go do some pushups or take some anabolic steroids or whatever it is you do before a fight and I'll sort this out."

"What I do is I relax," Brion said. "Prepare myself mentally for what is to come."

"Well you just go and do that. I'll let you see the final list for approval before I order the equipment."

"No, you don't have to do that. I leave that up to you and the experts. Just see that the outfitting is as complete as possible. I'll need some special equipment, but I'll arrange for that myself. All that I want right now is a detailed copy of the planetary survey. And a quiet spot to look at it."

"You have private quarters," Klart told him. "You'll find all the information you want waiting for you in the terminal there."

"Good. How soon can the equipment we need be readied?"

"Two, three hours in the most."

"We'll take ten. I want to sleep first." He looked at the distant planet again. "As soon as we have rested and are equipped I want to board our lifeship and put it into a low orbit, then take a closer look at the planet's surface. I'm very interested in just exactly what kind of animals those were that Hartig saw."

Brion had been deeply asleep when Lea opened the door, but he awoke instantly. She hesitated, blinking into the darkness, and he called out to her. "Come in. I'll turn on the light."

"Do you usually sleep with all your clothes on?" she asked. "And your boots as well?"

"It's called establishing a body image." He drew a large glass of water from the dispenser and sipped at it. "I'll be living in these clothes for some days, so they must be accepted as a part of my body. My body and my reflexes are my major defense, my most important weapon. I will be taking a knife as well. I have considered it carefully and I think the defense it will offer will be worth the gamble of taking it with me."

"What knife—and what gamble? I don't understand."

"The knife will have to be made of a mineral. It will be the only exception, the only object not of completely natural origin. These clothes are made of vegetable fibers, their buttons are carved from bone. My boots are of leather made from animal hide, sewn and glued together. I have no metal, nor do I wear anything made of artificial fibers."

"Not even the fillings in your teeth?" she asked, smiling.

"No, not even them." Brion was unsmiling and deadly serious. "All of the metallic fillings have been removed and have been replaced with ceramic inlays. The closer I resemble any other creature in the natural environment, the safer I will be. That is why the knife is a calculated risk." He turned so she could see the leather scabbard suspended at his side. From it he drew the long and transparent weapon and held it out for her inspection.

"It looks like glass. Is that what it is?"

He shook his head. "No, plasteel. A form of silicon that resembles glass in some ways, but it is stronger by a factor of one hundred since the molecules have been realigned to form a single giant crystal. It is virtually unbreakable and has an edge that will never dull. Since it is silicon, like sand, it should resemble sand to any detection apparatus. That is why I am taking the chance of having it with me."

Lea watched in silence as Brion put the weapon carefully away, arched his fingers, then stretched like a great cat. She could see the movement of his muscles beneath the fabric of his clothing, was aware of his strength that was more than something simply physical.

"I have a feeling that you can do it," she said. "I

doubt if anyone else could, not anyone else in this
entire spiral galaxy. Of course I still think that the
whole thing is pretty insane—although I also think
that it is probably the best chance we have of finding
out what is happening down there."

His reactions were so fast; it was something she
had never become accustomed to. His arms were
around her before she realized that he had moved;
the strength in his hands like steel inside flesh. He
kissed her quickly then stepped away. "Thank you.
With your understanding and belief I am more prepared now to do what must be done. Let's go to the
ship."

There was no ceremony involved in their depar-
ture. While Lea checked the loading lists, Brion
talked to the chief navigation officer, who then
computed and filed a number of orbits into the lifeship's computer for them. When the preparatory
work had been done, and all the checklists completed, they sealed the hatch. As soon as the signal
was received that they were ready, the computer
started the program that dropped them free of the
mother ship. Gas jets flared to rotate the lifeship,
then the main engines fired to put them into the
designated orbit. Selm-II grew larger and larger on
the screen before them.

"You're frightened," Brion said, covering her cold
hand with his large one.

"It doesn't take an empathetic to figure that one
out," she said, shivering and drawing close to him.
"This operation may have looked good on paper—
but the closer we get to that planet of no return
down there the more worried I get. Two good men,
both of them contact experts, have been killed down
there. The same thing is very likely to happen to us."

"I don't think so. We are far better prepared than they were. And it is their sacrifice that has supplied us with the information that we will need to survive. There's nothing to be concerned about at this time. You must force yourself to relax, to conserve your energy and resources for the moment when they will be needed. What we must do now is establish a low orbit and do a complete survey before looking for a place to set down. Until that time there is no danger."

The computer broke in, giving instant lie to his words.

"I have an atmospheric craft under observation. Its present course will pass beneath ours. Should I display?"

"Yes."

A small dot appeared on the screen moving slowly from left to right.

"Enlarge the image."

The moving speck swelled and became a thin metallic dart with swept-back wings. "What is its speed?" Brion asked, and a display appeared on the screen. "Mach 2.6. An advanced supersonic design, product of a highly developed technological culture. At that speed it will have limited fuel. If we can keep it in sight, we might be able to see where it lands . . ."

Lea finished the sentence for him. "And we also may stand a good chance of finding out just what is happening on this planet."

"Exactly . . ."

The image of the aircraft on the screen tilted up on one wing and dived sharply; the computer spoke in the same instant.

"*There is a digital radio broadcast emanating from the displayed plane. I am recording.*"

The image on the screen disappeared in a sudden explosion of flame. "What caused that blowup?" Brion said.

"*A surface to air missile. I detected its course just before the explosion.*"

Brion nodded grimly. "That aircraft must have detected it as well, that's why it took the sudden evasive action."

"And that broadcast—is it possible that the crew of the plane sent it out?"

"Yes, of course! If it was a scout ship it was in that particular area for some reason. When it was fired

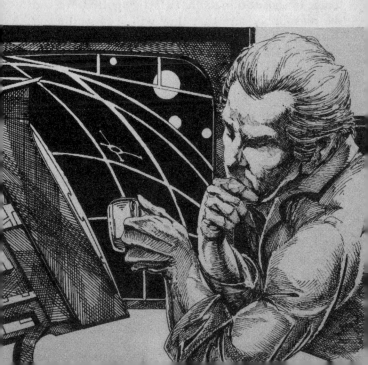

upon they took evasive action while reporting back to their base. And unless I am mistaken—here comes the response now." Brion pointed to the track suddenly displayed on the screen. "A ballistic missile, probably targeted on the ground defense missile site below. The war is still going on. So we know two more places where we don't want to go."

"The target site below—where something has just blown up with a spectacular explosion—and also the place where that missile was launched from that did all the damage."

"Exactly. Until we know what is happening on this planet we want to stay as far away as possible from any war zones. Now let's see if we can find some of those animals that Hartig spotted. We can be reasonably sure that they will keep well away from any battles or moving machinery. They took off when Hartig's ship landed, and I imagine they will stay as far away as possible from anything mechanical.

They found the site they were looking for on the eastern shore of the gigantic lake that they named the Central Sea. Moving dots were scattered over the grass plains that stretched from the foothills all the way to the lake shore. Under the highest resolution of the electronic telescope, it could be seen that these were grazing animals of some kind. The location of the herd was recorded as well as other herds along the shore. There appeared to be predators as well; they saw one group fleeing in panic from what appeared to be larger and faster pursuers. But in all their searching they found absolutely no sign at all of any kind of civilization.

"That's the area where I would like to drop," Brion said. "On the plain where all the herds are."

"What do you mean when you say 'drop'? Aren't we going to land this lifeship?"

"No. That's the last thing we want to do. You saw what happened to that aircraft. We don't want to get into radar range and alert their missiles. So I am going to compute a ballistic orbit that will drop me into the atmosphere at the correct spot."

"Won't it hurt just a little bit when you burn up, after impacting all that air waiting for you down there?"

Brion smiled. "I appreciate your concern. I'll be wearing a gravchute that will slow my fall. I've also removed all of the unessential metal fittings from the pressure suit, even substituted a plastic oxygen tank. There is only the slightest chance that I can be detected by ground radar—particularly since the area we have picked seems to be clear of constructions of any kind. As soon as I hit the ground I'll get rid of the gravchute along with the rest of the space gear."

"But you'll be stranded!"

"Hardly. I'll be in communication with you."

"Will you? Then you have invented an all-plastic radio?" Her attempt at humor failed dismally; there was only concern in her voice now.

"I intend to use these," Brion said, pulling a length of colored cloth from the pack at his side. "I've worked out a simple code. When I spread these panels on the ground you'll be able to see them clearly from space. As soon as I am down and it is daylight, I will lay out a message for you. As I move about I'll send you regular messages so you will know everything that is happening."

"It's dangerous . . ."

"Everything about this operation is dangerous.

But there is no other way that it can be done." He
turned back to the screen and examined the image
carefully, finally tapping his finger on the image.

"That's where I want to go. Close to the place
where the plains meet the hills. There will be wood-
land nearby for cover. If we time it right I can drop
during the night and reach the ground at dawn. I
will take shelter as soon as possible, then make my
observations. If these animals are what they appear
to be, wild native life forms, I can move on to the
next step in the observation."

"And that is going to be exactly what?"

"An approach on foot to one of the battle areas
. . ."

"You can't!"

"I'm sorry—but I must. There is very little we can
learn about machine warfare from a herd of wild
animals. The nearest wrecks are only about one-
hundred miles away from my drop zone. An easy
two or three day walk. I'll make daily reports as I go,
starting all messages with an 'X'. This regular form
does not occur in nature, so a computer scan will
locate and zero in on it for you. I'm going to get some
sleep now. Please wake me up an hour before I have
to leave."

The surface of Selm-II was lost in darkness below
when Brion eased himself into the airlock. Everything he would need after he had landed was now
sealed away in a thick plastic tube he had slung
across his back. The bulk of the gravchute rested
lightly on his massive shoulders, well strapped into
place. Lea watched him as he checked the fastening
on his pressure suit one last time; her hands were
clasped so tightly together that her knuckles were

white. He looked up and waved, but as he turned to leave she leaned forward and rapped on the front of his helmet. Brion unlocked the faceplate and swung it open. His expression was as calm as hers was perturbed.

"Yes?" he said.

For a moment she was silent, the only sound the hissing of oxygen from the helmet inlet. Then she leaned forward, standing on tiptoes, and kissed him firmly on the mouth. "I just wanted to wish you good luck. I'll see you soon?"

"Of course." He was smiling as he closed the faceplate again. Then he shuffled forward into the airlock and closed the inner door behind him; the indicator beside it flared red a moment later as the outer door opened.

Brion waited then, long minutes, staring out in the vacuum of space, until the computer signalled that the right moment had come. The instant the green light flashed on the control panel he launched himself forward and out of the ship.

Lea sat at the viewscreen and watched his falling body, pinpointed by the flare of braking rockets, until it dropped behind and vanished from sight.

FIVE

Barehanded Into Hell

Brion dropped down into the black hole of the night. There was no sensation of motion in his free fall, although logically he knew that his speed was accelerating with every passing moment. Yet he appeared to be unmoving, alone in space, surrounded by the stars, with the dark disc of the night-shrouded planet below him. The planet itself was surrounded by a corona of light where the occluded sunlight was refracted by the atmosphere. It was brighter on the eastern side where sunrise was on its way. Despite his apparent lack of motion, Brion knew that he was hurtling downward in a carefully computed arc towards a precise spot on the surface below, falling towards the sunrise. The microcomputer in the gravchute on his back was ticking off the seconds leading up to that moment of arrival. From time to time he felt slight tugs on his harness as his fall was slowed by precisely measured amounts to conform to that program.

It was only because of all of his years of training that he managed to keep his thoughts calm, to hold at bay the close-pressing fear that would cause his body to react and send the adrenalin circulating uselessly through his veins. The time for action would come after the landing; the time now was for contemplation. He sank quietly into a relaxed state of halfawareness, letting his body drop into the seemingly endless fall, ignoring the slight tugs on his harness that soon strengthened into a continual pull. The first traces of thickening atmosphere brushed against his suit. The fall continued.

Sudden light burst into his eyes as the sun cleared the horizon. He stirred and flexed his muscles; it would be time soon. Although it was sunrise at his altitude, the land below was still filled with night. An all-prevading grayness suddenly replaced the light as he dropped through a thick belt of cloud— then out of it again to fall towards the dimly lit landscape below.

Safe so far. There were no missiles—or aircraft. But he was well aware of the easily detectable metal in his equipment. He could be a blip on radar screens at this instant, missiles could be rising in his direction. He ached to be on the ground and free of the revealing metal. Twisting in the harness Brion looked down between his feet at the grassy plain that was hurtling towards him. He knew that he was falling too fast—but speed was his only defense. If there were radar detectors out there he had to be on their screens for the least possible time. Which meant that he had to fall just as far and as fast as he could, waiting to brake his fall at the last possible instant. This moment was fast approaching. The ground was closer, almost upon him—now!

A twist of the control switch sent power surging through the gravchute and the harness bit deep into his thighs. He was still falling too fast—he had to feed in more power. The harness creaked with the strain. Ease off. Now—full on!

His feet struck the ground hard so that he had to fall and roll end over end among the tall grass. Then all he could do was lie still for long seconds with the wind knocked from his body. He willed his limbs to move but at first there was no response.

It took a determined effort to pull himself to his knees, then to weakly draw himself up, to stand at last. To then do all of the other things that could not wait, that must to be done at once.

With the power off, and the harness released, the gravchute crashed heavily to the ground. Brion tore open the pressure suit and stripped it off, making sure that the helmet was still attached to it, the oxygen bottle as well. Right, everything in order.

Now—rush but don't rush. There was just enough light in the gray of the dawn to see what he was doing. Pull open the carrier tube slung below the gravchute and shake out the knife and bag that he would be taking with him. The bag was sticking, tear it free, right, both of them out now. Get rid of everything else. Wrap the harness of the gravchute around the equipment that he was jettisoning. Double check to be sure that everything was secure. Good. Had he forgotten anything? No, everything was in place.

Brion twisted the gravchute power on full so that the bundle was torn from his grasp, knocking him aside as it hurtled skyward. It began to shrink as it rose, until it had vanished from sight almost completely. There was a flash of light from the faceplate as it caught the rising sun high above. Then even this was gone.

Brion let his breath out in an unconscious sigh of relief. He was on the ground and he was alive. The fall to the planet's surface had been successful so he could put all thought of the descent behind him. Now was the time for the real work to begin.

While he bent over to retrieve his knife, Brion turned in a slow circle. He secured the sheath to his belt by touch, clumsily, since all of his attention was focussed now on the brightening landscape.

There was grass on all sides of him. Tall grass that was beginning to whisper and nod in the dawn breeze, undulating away from him in waves. Close by was a rocky mound, then a grove of trees on the western horizon, while beyond the grove were the rising foothills that lead up to the tree covered mountains beyond. Their summits were already being touched with fire from the rising sun.

Sudden movement caught his attention. There, in the direction of the lake. Brion crouched slowly, until only his eyes were above the grass. He could see a herd of creatures moving in his direction, grazing as they came. He remained as motionless as a rock, only his hands moving, drifting slowly downwards as he retrieved his pack and slung it by the strap over his shoulder.

Harsh cries shrilled suddenly in the air above him. Brion's eyes snapped up to see the flock of birds circling close, then landing. No, they weren't birds at all, but flying reptiles of some sort. Instead of feathers they had leathery membranes stretched between the thin bones of their outspread wings. Their skins glistened in the sunlight, red and orange; the creatures heads were split by gaping jaws that appeared to be filled with needle teeth. Still calling out harshly they dropped lower until they sank out of sight in the sea of grass.

The grazing creatures were closer and Brion could now see them clearly. They were lizardoids as well. Their hairless skins were dun-colored; perfect camouflage in the dried grass. They moved warily on their long running legs, raising their heads often and opening their nostril flaps to smell the air. There must be predators about—and Brion had a feeling that they would also be reptilian.

The herd was aware of something now. The creatures had stopped grazing and were standing, frozen, with their nostrils flared wide. Perhaps another animal was approaching. Though they had caught its smell, it was still concealed from sight in the deep grass. A drama of life and death was about to be played out close by him.

Brion realized with sudden shock that he might be more than a simple spectator, when he noticed that all of the creatures appeared to be staring in his direction. Had they seen him? He sank down even lower to avoid their gaze, empathetically feeling the thin undercurrent of their emotions. Fear. Fear that replaced all other sensations. His empathetic sense was normally sensitive only to human beings, but strong emotions from other animals occasionally seeped through. He was well aware of the creatures fear now—and something else, something stronger . . .

Brion sprang to his feet, tearing his knife from its sheath, spinning about just in time to see the dark form that hurtled towards him. High-pitched

shrieking tore at his ears. Something hard crashed
into his shoulder as he dived aside, spinning him
about, numbing his arm so that he almost dropped
the knife. He fumbled it into his left hand and saw
the creature rising above him again, jaws agape,
rows of teeth glistening.

It was falling upon him with its full weight as he
plunged the knife into its throat. With a strangled
screech it collapsed, crushing him to the ground.
The creature shuddered convulsively once and then
was still. Warm liquid bathed Brion's arm, the
beast's blood or his own, he could not tell. Bracing
his feet against the animal's body he pushed himself
free, looking around desperately at the same time to
see if there were more of the things about.

There had been just the one. He stood, gasping
with the effort; the only motion visible now was the
herd of grazing creatures which was rapidly bounding out of sight. Looking down Brion saw that his
arms were drenched with green blood—that was
surely not his own!

Beside him on the ground the unmoving beast lay
stretched out, motionless and dead. It's yard-long
and tooth-lined jaws were open and gaping, its eyes
staring sightlessly at him. The dead predator had
short, claw-tipped forelegs, while its rear legs were
immense, to give it speed when it attacked. The
creature's wrinkled hide was a mottled and ugly
brown tinged with purple. The color of the shadows
Brion realized. A killing machine. It was no wonder
the other animals had been so wary.

Brion was suddenly very tired. He dropped down
heavily onto the beast's flank, then wiped the gore
from his fingers onto its skin. He drank deeply from
his pressed wood water bottle, then could only sit

and breathe heavily while he waited for his strength to return. Not a very auspicious beginning to his investigation; he had almost been killed by the first creature he had met. Almost—but not quite. The knife was sharp and well balanced, his reflexes as fast as ever. He would not be surprised as easily as this again.

But at least he was down on the planet and relatively safe for the moment. It was time for his next step. Up to now he had been worried only about survival. First there had been the necessity of evading the missiles in the air and the war machines on the ground. Well he had done all that. And had survived the predator's attack as well. The first part of the mission had been accomplished. The next thing he had to do was report his safe arrival before he moved on.

This area was as good as any on the plain; well away from the trees and clearly visible from space. The grass had been trampled by the animals, but there still wasn't a flattened area big enough to lay out the message. However there was the stony mound nearby and this was not covered by the high grass. He clambered up onto it and opened his bag, pulling out the bundle of colored cloth panels. Although he knew that there was nothing for him to see he could not stop himself from looking up at the empty blue sky. The lifeship was there in orbit, invisible to him although he knew Lea would be able to see him clearly under electronic magnification. He had to smile to himself as he waved his arms widely; it was a victory gesture and he felt the better for doing it. Then he bent to the task of arranging the panels to make the first signal.

First the 'X' to draw the computer's attention in

case he was not under observation. Then the rest of the message. The code was a simple one that he had worked out and memorized. 'I' to indicate that he had landed safely—if she had watched the encounter with the attacking reptile she might very well be having some doubts about that. He stood aside for a short period so the signal could be recorded, then added a panel to turn the 'I' into a 'T' to show that he was proceeding with the operation as planned, and would signal again as soon as possible. He had to weigh down the cloth with stones to hold it flat, since the dawn breeze was growing stronger as the sun rose higher in the sky and heated up the ground.

From the top of the mound the surrounding countryside was clearly visible. The grazing saurians had outrun their panic and were now grazing along the shore of the lake. The route he had to take to the nearest battlefield was an easy one, simply proceed west along the shore of the lake until he reached the spot. A simple walk that would give him a chance to examine the countryside and the animals as he went. It was time to go. He refolded the panels and stowed them away. Then, with the sun warm on his back, he started west.

At midday he stopped to rest and eat. The freeze-dried rations would supply all the energy he needed for a number of days—but were as tasteless as dried cardboard. He washed them down with water, then shook the bottle to see how much remained. Enough for the rest of the day, but it would need refilling before nightfall. He would take care of that later, well before dark. After that he would move away from the lake and find some shelter among the rocks or trees for the night. The single predator he had met had given him a healthy respect for the wildlife on this planet. He put the wrapping from the food and the water bottle back into the bag and climbed to his feet, stretching.

At first the sound was so tiny and distant he took it for the whine of an insect—but it grew quickly, louder and louder. He dived sideways into the cover of the deep grass as he recognized it. A jet engine. It was missing, then catching again as though it were in trouble. It came out of the sun, a white contrail with the black dot of an aircraft leading it. Twisting and turning as though the pilot was avoiding something. The course turned again, bending in his direction, passing almost directly overhead and hurtling on with a roar.

Then disappearing in a sudden burst of flame that expanded instantly into a white cloud. Something black arced out and down towards the ground, falling no more than a mile away from him. It struck and sent up a cloud of dust just as the rumbling sound of the aerial explosion finally reached his ears.

Brion stood slowly and looked towards the settling dust. This had been too close by far. Was it an accident—or had the appearance of the plane something to do with him? Impossible, he was being paranoid, it was just a coincidence that the incident had occurred so close to him. But if it were just a coincidence, why did he have the cold touch of fear when he thought of approaching the wreckage? His sense of survival wanted him to stay away. But for the sake of this mission he had to investigate the site. The pilot's body might be there, or evidence of some kind. He really had no choice. The dust cloud had settled now and the plain was featureless again. But he had noted the direction. Without further thought he started towards it.

The crater was a dark blotch in the sea of grass. Brion approached it cautiously, crawling the last few yards on his belly. When he peered slowly over the edge he could see crushed metal at the bottom of the deep crater. It was one of the aircraft's wings. There were no identity markings on it that he could see, even when he dropped down beside it. The surface of the wreckage was still warm and he moved around it gingerly. Fragments of metal had been torn away by the impact and he turned them over with his knife, one by one. His diligence was rewarded finally when he found a twisted identity plate. With the lettering still visible!

However there was one thing wrong with this. Although the letters were clear, the few words between the numbers were in a language he had never seen before. It was a clue he could not unravel at the moment—yet it could not be ignored. He considered prying the plate off, then realized that carrying any metal with him, no matter how small the fragment, would be foolhardy. In the end he used the point of his knife to scratch a copy onto his waterbottle. He had a record of it at least.

The investigation had taken him away from the lake, so when he started walking again he angled back towards its shore. He could see at least three herds of beasts grazing close to the water and he moved slowly in their direction. His water was gone now and it was getting late; he would refill it where the creatures had gone to drink.

Some of the open forest pushed out into the plain ahead. It must have served as cover for predators because sudden panic ran through the grazing herd that he was following. Some of them even stampeded in his direction and he stood still as they rushed by. Their long legs gave them a good turn of speed and they were past in a moment, followed closely by the younger and slower members of the herd. One of the last of the creatures was a heavyset male with a spread of barbed horns. It shook these menacingly in Brion's direction, then trundled on when he made no threatening motions. When they had all passed Brion backtracked them through the paths they had trampled in the grass, stepping around the streams of pungent dung.

He moved very warily, his knife in his hand, looking in all directions and listening keenly at the same time. Stopping instantly when he saw a dark form on the ground ahead, half concealed by the high grass.

It was a dead herbivore, its head towards him, mouth still gaping in the panic of death. Its killer wa⁻ nowhere to be seen. Carefully, a step at a time, Brion moved forward until he could see that nothing was concealed in the grass near the animal. The creature that had killed it must be long gone. Brion still kept his knife drawn as he circled around the body. The creature's throat had been torn open, very cleanly too; he couldn't have done it any better with his own knife.

He stopped, frozen. The wound was too clean. And so was the larger wound on the beast's flank. Not a wound really, but an excision. One of the rear legs was gone.

Cut off cleanly at the joint.

No animal had done this with teeth or claws.

It could only have been done by the kind of animal that carried a very sharp knife.

Brion looked up from the kill towards the concealing darkness of the nearby copse of trees. Were there eyes watching him from concealment there? Was there an intelligent life form on this planet? Or could they be human eyes?

SIX

Alien Encounter

This was a time for thought, not action. As soon as Brion saw the cleanly cut flesh he knew that. With deliberate motions he slipped his knife back into its sheath on his hip, then just as slowly lowered himself to a sitting position on the ground. Looking out towards the lake like this he was not obviously watching the grove of trees—but he could see it clearly out of the corner of his eyes. The only motion was the nodding of the grass before the wind, the same wind that was ruffling the surface of the water.

Intelligent creatures had killed the creature at his side. Men, or aliens, with knives, who had butchered the body then fled with the meat. Whoever they were must have seen him coming and hurried to the safety of the trees. They were probably there now, watching him. He relaxed his muscles and tried to reach out and make contact with them, but his empathetic sense was a crude tool at any distance; he was aware of people's emotions when they were close by, but the sensitivity faded quickly as they moved away. He concentrated now, reaching out. Something, a living creature. That was all he could tell about it. It was so dimly felt that it could be anything, a human being—or perhaps an alien, or even the simple awareness of an animal like the one lying dead before him. It was calm sensation, whatever it was; perhaps it would be easier to read if it were made clearer and stronger.

Without warning Brion suddenly sprang high into the air, shrieking wildly as he jumped. Dropping back to the ground he began to shuffle around the animal's body, shouting aloud as he did. He made one complete circle then eased himself down to a sitting position on the ground again, smiling cheerfully to himself.

Oh yes, there was something out there all right. And not an alien life form or one of the local reptiles. The response had been that of a human being—one who had been very startled when Brion had suddenly lept up and screamed aloud. There was a single person there, a man, watching him, unseen behind the concealing foliage of the trees. Possessed by fear. That was the emotion he had projected at the sudden sound. He was afraid of Brion.

Despite his overriding fear, the man had to be contacted. But just how could this be accomplished? Brion's eyes were focused on the carcass beside him. This might provide a way. As unappetizing as the flesh of this creature appeared, with its thick green blood, it must be edible by human beings. Because the hiding man was human, that fact was as unarguable as his human emotions. He had slaughtered the animal for food, but had fled with only a single limb when Brion had appeared. A friendly gesture of some kind was in order.

Brion carved through the hip joint of the remaining rear leg, severing it cleanly from the body. He picked it up and carried it extended before him so it could be clearly seen, then he walked slowly towards the trees. Being careful not to move in the direction of the hidden observer. When he reached the first tree a single slash severed a thick branch and, then, after making an incision behind the leg tendon, he impaled the joint on its end.

Step one. If the watcher took the meat it meant they had opened communication of a sort. This would be a good moment to refill his waterbottle. The animals had trodden paths to the lakeside and he followed them to the shore, pushing his way out through the reeds until the water reached his waist. It was clear and unmuddied here and, after tasting it, he filled the bottle. The sun was nearing the horizon when he returned. A flock of scavenging flying lizards was perched on the corpse, tearing at the flesh with their needle-fanged jaws. They reluctantly flapped off, screaming shrilly, when he came close. The sun was low on the horizon and he had to shield his eyes with his hand as he looked into it. The haunch of meat was gone—but the hidden watcher was still there. Now all that Brion could do was wait. But not near the dead animal. That would not be too wise. The scavengers still circled above him, shrieking continuously, and would surely draw other and larger scavengers to the kill. The trees should offer him some protection. He went slowly to the end of the copse furthest from the man who was watching him, his movements clear in the failing light.

As night fell Brion was aware of the man moving further away among the trees, until the sensation of his presence was just the slightest touch at the farthermost fringe of his empathetic senses. He obviously did not want to be surprised during the night. Neither did Brion. He smoothed out the fallen leaves next to the bole of the largest tree, then fell asleep with the knife clasped firmly in his hand. It was a light sleep during which he was aware always of his surrounding. He woke once, peering into the darkness, as some night creature crept by. It sensed his presence and gave him a wide berth. Nothing else disturbed him during the night and he awoke, refreshed, at the first light of dawn.

The hunter was still here—and still watching. Brion could feel the surge of emotion from the man when Brion moved out into the plain away from the trees. There was still fear there—but curiosity as well. Brion knew that he would have to control his impatience. The next step was up to the hidden observer.

Waiting was not easy to do. By noon Brion was bored with simply sitting still and hoping for something to happen. Herds of the grazing creatures moved by in the distance, the sun rose higher into the cloudless sky—and nothing changed. He ate some of his rations at midday, washing them down with lake water. To control his impatience he tried composing a poem about the landscape, but found this even more boring than the waiting. Then he played mental chess with himself, but lost track of black's twentieth move and abandoned this effort as

well. By midafternoon he had had enough. The other
man was apparently happy just to lie in hiding and
watch him. That was going to change. Brion stood
and stretched, then turned and began to walk slowly
in the other's direction.

There was a surge of fear so sharp and clear that
Brion could pick out the exact hiding place of the
man, behind the trunk of a large fallen tree. He
stopped instantly and raised his empty hands over
his head. The sensation of wild panic faded but the
fear remained, completely wiping out the curiosity
that had kept the man hiding and watching all day.
There were mixed emotions now, for greed was
there behind the fear as well. Brion took a step
closer, and when he did fear completely overwhelmed greed—the man fled. When Brion walked
over to his hiding place he understood what the
conflicting emotions had meant. The two haunches
of meat had been left behind. Too heavy to carry,
thrown aside in panic. Brion bent and picked them
up, one in each hand, carrying them easily on his
broad shoulders as he moved out on the man's trail.

It was soon obvious that the man was heading for
the thicker forest and the hills beyond. When Brion
was sure of his direction he made his way out onto
the plain where he could move faster, running along
beside the trees to get ahead of the other man. The
going was easier this way, and even though he was
burdened by the meat he easily outreached the other
man. Then cut back into the trees ahead of him.
There was a game trail here through the thickening
forest and the other was still coming in this direction, perhaps along the trail. It was a good place to
wait. Brion put down his burden, scarcely breathing

hard, and waited, facing back down the trail. Aware of the other's approach as well as his fear and growing fatigue.

They saw each other at the same instant and the sharp spurt of horror sent the hunter's arm forward in sudden reflex. Brion had only a glimpse of the spear coming towards him as he hurled himself to one side. The point buried itself in the tree trunk beside him. The hunter crouched and drew his knife as Brion climbed slowly to his feet. Without taking his eye from the other, Brion reached out and pulled the spear free and let it drop to the ground. Then, ever so slowly, he drew his own knife and dropped it beside the spear. Waves of fright were still radiating from the other man. Brion waited in silence until the

quick rush of fear had lessened before he spoke in what he hoped was a reassuring voice.

"I mean you no harm. Here is my knife—and here is the meat. Let us be friends."

The other could not understand him, but the calm tone of Brion's voice seemed to be having some effect. Brion pointed to the meat and the weapons, still speaking reassuredly, then moved aside off the path, but still making sure the man could see him. When he was a good dozen yards away he stopped and sat down with his back to a tree, waiting for the other to move. Savoring the radiated emotions as the panic slowly ebbed away to be partially replaced by curiosity. The man took one cautious step forward, then another, coming out into the sunlight. They looked at each other with mutual curiosity.

The hunter was human enough, but scrawny and short, scarcely up to Brion's shoulder. His long hair was matted; filthy strands of it were hanging lankly over his face. He was dressed in lizard skins, with more of the skins bound crudely about his feet. As he came forward he looked at Brion's clothes and boots with awe, his eyes wide and his mouth hanging loosely open. Brion smiled and made encouraging noises as the other bent over the weapons. He tried not to reveal his feelings when he saw his knife in the man's hand. He was turning it over and over, wondering at it, reacting with a spurt of fear when the sharp-edged weapon cut his thumb. He put it into his mouth and sucked on it, the gesture strangely childlike. Only after the pain and burst of fear had ebbed away did he bend down and use the knife to saw off a rough chunk of meat from one of the haunches.

Brion felt a happy throb of success when the hunter slowly extended the raw gobbet of flesh in his direction. He nodded and smiled in return and started slowly forward, his hand outstretched. As he came close fear spurted again and the man dropped the meat and retreated a few paces. Brion stopped at once and waited patiently until the other had calmed down. Only then did he advance, step by careful step, to bend and pick up the meat. He chewed a bit—it was loathsome—but he smiled and rubbed his stomach, making happy noises.

Most of the fear was gone now and the hunter was smiling as well, first tentatively, then broadly, rubbing his stomach just as Brion had done, imitating the sounds he had made at the same time.

Contact had been established at last.

SEVEN

First Contact

Now that peaceful contact had been established it seemed as though all fear had been drained from the hunter. Brion was empathetically aware of this, though he found it hard to believe at first. This was a grown man—yet his reactions seemed oddly child-ish. His first fear at seeing a stranger had been held at bay by his later curiosity. Then, instead of seeking escape he had stayed to watch Brion's arrival, had even remained the night. First greed, then fear again—as though he could not feel more than one strong emotion at a time. Childlike. Now he chattered happily to himself as he examined Brion's clothes and boots, drank water noisily from the bottle, chewed on the dried rations—then spat them out with distaste. All of this done with an unquestioning and childlike acceptance of the novel situation.

There had not even been a trace of apprehension

when Brion, during the course of showing the man
the contents of the bag, had idly picked up his knife
and slipped it back into its sheath. The hunter had
not even noticed the action. He was too fascinated
by everything that Brion possessed to take even
minimal safety precautions.

It did not take Brion long to realize that this man's
culture appeared to be as primitive as his simple
and unquestioning acceptance of their new relationship. His artifacts were crude stone age. The
spearpoint was a sharp flake of glassy volcanic rock
tied crudely onto the end of the shaft. The hunter's
knife was shaped from stone as well. The lizard skins
he wore for clothing were completly uncured—that
was obvious from their smell—and the only decoration or non-utilitarian item he possessed was the
saurian skull. This repulsive object, with its decaying skin still in place, was worn as a helmet.

When the man's first curiosity had been satisfied,
Brion made an attempt to communicate with him.
It was almost completely unsuccessful. After end-
lessly pointing at himself and speaking his name,
then pointing at the hunter and making enquiring
noises, Brion did discover that the man was called
Vjer. Or Vjr, a single explosive sound completly
lacking in vowels. He pronounced Brion more like
'Bran' or 'Brrn', again free of vowel sounds. And this
was the limit of their communication. Vjer soon lost
interest in words and refused to learn any more of
Brion's, or to speak any of his own for Brion to learn.
His attention span was very limited. He grew thirsty
and emptied the water bottle, spilling more than he
drank. Later, when he became hungry he hacked off
some of the green lizard flesh, ignoring the fact it
was already infested with blowflies, chewing and

swallowing it raw with noisy satisfaction. Brion found everything about the man difficult to understand.

Vjer was a primitive, nothing more. With his empathetic sense, Brion could tell that he was not simulating. He was exactly what he appeared to be; an unimaginative and simple stone age primitive. Yet this planet was dominated by two warring forces who were locked in what appeared to be a continuous battle, using the most sophisticated weaponry. Where did Vjer fit into all this? Was he an outcast of some kind? A refugee from the fighting? There was no way of telling without opening some channel of communication. Was he alone or was he part of a group? What was the next step to be?

It was Vjer who decided that. He had quietly dozed off after finishing the bloody gobbet of meat. Squatting on his heels, he was instantly and deeply asleep, his actions more like those of an animal than a human being. He woke up just as suddenly, squinting up at the sky and muttering something incomprehensible. He must have reached a decision of some kind because he used his crude knife to hack a length of tough vine from one of the trees. With this he lashed the two haunches of meat together, then grunted as he hoisted them to his shoulder. With the knife in one hand, the spear in the other, he started down the path—then stopped as though he had remembered something.

"Brrn," he said, chuckling to himself. "Brrn, Brrn!" Then he turned back and continued on his way.

"Wait," Brion called out. "I want to come with you."

He started to follow the man—and stopped at the

sudden wave of fear that washed over him. Vjer was shivering, his spear shaking in his hand so great was his panic. He backed slowly away, then halted again when Brion made as if to follow, radiating unhappiness, great tears forming in his eyes.

"Well I guess you don't want me to go with you," Brion said, in what he hoped was a soothing tone. "But we'll meet again. You'll be up in these hills somewhere and shouldn't be hard to find."

Vjer's panic faded when Brion made no move to follow him a second time. He backed away among the trees, then turned and hurried off as fast as he could under the burden of the meat. When he was well out of sight Brion turned and went in the opposite direction, back to the plain. He made a quick detour to refill his waterbottle then began trotting back along the track he had taken the previous day. He had a fixed objective in mind now. The visit to the battlefield could wait—the longer that he put off personal contact with the deadly enemy the better. There would be time enough to do that after he had managed to communicate with Vjer. It might be possible, though it was surely a long shot, that Vjer could tell him enough about the war so he would not have to make the dangerous journey.

The crater was clearly visible in the open plain and he made his way towards it, stopping when he was about a hundred yards distant. He then trampled in a circle to flatten the grass, so that his signal panels could be seen. It was only a few minutes before the area was flat enough to enable him to spread out the pieces of thin cloth. He used chunks of dirt that had been blasted from the crater to hold them in place. After laying out the 'X' he paused and counted slowly to one hundred. This should give the lifeship's computer, in orbit high above, enough time to identify and zero in on his signal.

When he was sure he was being observed, Brion spelled out a 'V' and another 'X', followed by two 'I's'. Then he sat back, sipped at his waterbottle, and waited.

The signal was clear enough. *Land. At this place. Soonest.* Right now the lifeship should be computing its orbit. Considering its present altitude, the ship should be on the ground within an hour, two at the most. Brion waited a few minutes, then gathered up all of the signal panels, except for the 'X', and stowed them away. When this task was finished he walked off for a quarter of a mile and sat down to

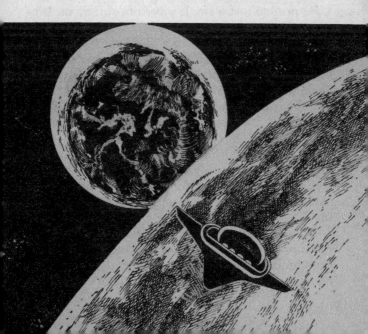

wait. Computers were very literal and the ship would land precisely where it had been instructed to. He had no intention of being on that spot.

But the longer he sat there, thinking about the situation, the more concerned he became. This mission was suddenly becoming very dangerous again. The lifeship would have to set down some time, there was no way to avoid that. And this spot was about the safest that could be found, the farthest away from any of the battle sites. Doubly safe because if there were metal detectors at work they might be confused by the wing of the destroyed aircraft. If the computers kept track of such things they would have logged this location as harmless. But all of this was just speculation. They would have to rely on a little luck as well.

He needed just a single piece of equipment. If he worked fast he could board, find what he needed, then get out—and have Lea and the ship spaceborne again within two minutes. He hoped that it would be enough time. Once the lifeship was safely away he would leave the equipment under the shattered metal wing and beat a quick retreat himself. If the equipment were still undisturbed by morning he would retrieve it, then go looking for Vjer.

By the time he first heard the distant rumble of jets overhead the sun had dropped close to the horizon, where it glowed ruddily through a thin bank of cloud. He looked up to see a tiny point of light burning down. It was far brighter than the setting sun, and grew rapidly into a tower of flame that dropped the lifeship safely to the ground. It touched down, right onto the 'X', incinerating it neatly, and he was running towards it even as the motors were still cutting out. The airlock ground open and a flexible ladder rattled down to the ground just as he reached its side.

Brion seized the rungs and began pulling himself up, hand over hand, not wasting time trying to set his boots into place on the flapping length of ladder. His arms worked as smoothly as pistons to haul him up the side of the ship and into the airlock. Lea was just turning from the controls when he appeared behind her, seizing her in his solid embrace, kissing her soundly before releasing her.

"It's wonderful to see you he said," turning and diving towards the storage racks. "It's been interesting but lonely, I want the HLP—here it is! Goodbye. Get this ship back into orbit as soon as I am clear."

He skidded to a stop because she was standing in front of the lock barring his exit. Blazing with anger.

"That's enough, my lightning lover. It's time we had a chat—"

"There is no time. You must get out of the way, get back into orbit, we could be attacked at any instant . . ."

"Shut up. Go get a remote controller. I'll wait for you on the ground."

Lea had picked up a heavy bag, turned and started down the ladder while he was still trying to think of an answer. Should he order her back, force her inside if she refused, try to argue with her, convince her that what she was doing was dangerous? All these thoughts rushed through his mind, to be replaced by the realization that none of them would do any good. They must breed for firm-mindedness on Earth because once she had decided what to do there was no altering the course of events. He bowed to the inevitable, even admitting to himself that having her with him was infinitely superior to being alone . . .

This was taking too much time! He jumped to the control panel and tore the remote controller from its socket; its ready light switching on automatically. He clipped it onto his belt next to the HLP as he dived into the airlock and dropped headlong down the ladder, jumping the last few yards to the ground. Stabbing at the buttons on the controller. He could hear the inner door of the lock slam shut as the ladder clattered back up into the ship. He ran.

Lea had not waited for him, knowing his superior turn of speed. Though she was running as fast as she could he overhauled her quickly, going two yards to her one. He scooped her up in passing and thundered on, not slowing in the slightest. When he heard the jets ignite he dropped to the ground, his body between her and the blast. Putting his arm around her as the ground rumbled and shook and a heated cloud of dust enveloped them. Lea sat up, coughing, wiping at her eyes.

"You stupid, musclebound caveman—do you realize that you almost cooked us with that lightning takeoff?"

"Not really," he said, smiling, rolling onto his back with his head cradled in his arms looking up at the receding flame of the lifeship. They were safe, at least for the moment. "I knew I could be clear of the blast with at least three seconds to spare. Allowing seven seconds for the lock mechanism . . . I felt that!"

"How wonderful!" Lea said, kicking him in the side again, just as hard as she could. The toe of her boot merely bounced off his rock-hard muscle, but the moment of protest gave her immense satisfaction. Brion grunted with surprise, then rolled over and sprang to his feet. Lea smiled up at him sweetly. "Well here we are, alone at last on this strange planet. What do we do next?"

Brion started to protest—then burst out laughing. She would never cease to amaze him. He unclipped the two instruments from his belt. "Are you wearing anything metallic—or is there any metal in that pack?"

"Negative to both. I planned this little expedition with care."

"Very good. There is a stand of heavy grass concealing a ditch, just over there. Go to it and I'll join you as soon as I get rid of these."

He loped back to the crater and jumped into it, carefully putting the two pieces of equipment under the twisted metal of the wing, whistling happily through his teeth. Almost done. It looked like they were getting away with it.

Lea was already under cover when he dropped down into concealment beside her. "Isn't it about time you told me just what is happening?" she said.

"You should not have done this. You should have remained safely in the ship."

"Why? The thing can fly itself as you have just proved. And two heads will be better than one now that you have found some of the natives. There is no other reason to want a Heuristic Language Processor in such a hurry, is there? In any case, the deed has been done. I'm here, our transportation is back in orbit—so what do we do next?"

She was right. What was done was done; Brion

had trained himself to always accept the reality of a situation that could not be changed. He pointed towards the tree-covered hills that bordered the plain.

"We stay under cover here until we're sure that there is no military interest in us. Then we go up into those hills and look for a simple-minded and filthy primitive whom I met. If we are lucky maybe we can find some of his friends as well. Once he has located them we are going to talk to them with the HPL to see if we can't get some answers to all those questions we have about this planet."

EIGHT

A Deadly Surprise

The hush of the evening was broken only by the hum of insects, the occasional distant cries of the flying reptiles. Brion felt the knot of tension lessen and vanish with the realization that they had not been observed, that there would be no retaliation for the landing. But as he relaxed, the sensation of tension was instantly replaced by one of hunger; it had been a long time between meals. He dug one of the dehydrated ration bars from his bag and peeled off the covering with a growing feeling of distaste.

"Not exactly a steak dinner, is it?" Lea said, seeing his expression.

"You can live forever on these things, though it's not much of a life. And, please, don't let me even think about steaks."

Lea swung her pack around and opened the top flap.

"I only mentioned it because I brought you one."
She smiled innocently at his dumbfounded expression. "It's a recipe I read once in a historical cookbook. It was recommended for attending the races in the winter, whatever that meant." She began to strip plastic wrappings from a large bundle. "Very simple to do really. You cut an entire loaf of bread down the middle and put a thick, hot, broiled steak into it and pour all the meat juices onto it before you close it up. After that you sort of press it so the bread absorbs the juices and . . ."

She held up flattened loaf and Brion growled deep in his throat as he reached out for it. He bit off the corner and chewed on it slowly with a blissful expression. "Lea, you are a wonder," he said, muffledly around the mouthful.

"I know it—and I'm glad you found it out as well. Now tell me about your smelly native."

Brion did not speak again until a good third of the massive sandwich had been consumed. With the first pangs of hunger reduced, he finished the rest more slowly and appreciatively as he talked.

"He's as simple as a child—but he's not a child. His name is Vjer, or something sounding very much like that. When I first confronted him he was terrified, but once he accepted me the fear vanished completely. It was simply unbelievable the way it happened. Like throwing a switch. But later, when I started to follow him, he became so upset that he actually cried. I let him go on alone after that, because I'm sure that I'll have no trouble finding him again."

"Is he some sort of mental deficient—an outcast perhaps?"

"There's a chance, but I don't think so. If you consider him in relation to his environment, you must admit that he is basically adapted for survival. He successfully tracked and killed one of the herbivores, and seemed perfectly happy to eat it raw. When he left he took the meat with him back to whatever camp or settlement he lives in. But there is really no point in theorizing at this time. We don't have enough facts to make even an educated guess. We are going to have to find him and learn his language, then let him answer our questions for himself." Brion glanced at the sun that was just slipping below the horizon. "This is as good a place as any to spend the night. We'll leave the equipment in the crater for the night, then go on at dawn."

"That's fine by me. There has been more than enough excitement for one day as far as I'm concerned." She took an insulated sleeping bag from her pack and spread it on the ground. "It's all right for you to travel rough, perhaps you're used to it. But I appreciate some of the more sophisticated pleasures—such as a warm bed. I also brought some sandwiches for my own dinner. And some wine in biodegradable container. You can share the wine as long as you don't think it is too sophisticated."

"I gratefully accept. I am really beginning to believe that your planet Earth really is the home of mankind."

"Womankind. You aren't getting this kind of service from any men that I have noticed.

They both slept well—until Brion woke suddenly during the night. Something had disturbed him, but he had no memory of what it was. He lay quietly looking up at the stars. He had noted the major constellations the night before, so now he could work out the time from their movement. It was well after midnight, just a few hours before dawn. There was no moon, Selm-II didn't have one, but the ground was bathed in soft light from the stars. This solar system was somewhere close to the center of the galaxy so that myriad stars burned down from the wide belt that spanned the sky above.

What had disturbed him? The night was quiet, so still that he could hear Lea's soft and regular breathing. Had he sensed emotions then? He reached out and was barely able to detect something. At the very edge of his perception. It was human. And feeling a single emotion. Hatred. Blind hatred, and rage, and the desire for death. It wasn't a single person either, but was coming from more than one source.

Directed at him.

Brion rolled over slowly and shook Lea awake, his finger resting lightly across her lips when he saw her blink and open her eyes. He put his lips against her ear and spoke in a quiet whisper.

"We're going to have some company soon. Better get your things packed together and be ready to move." He was aware of the sudden tenseness and fear in her body as she pushed herself up on her elbows.

"What's happening?"

"I can't be sure yet. But I can feel them, people out there in the darkness. They are coming this way. I can't tell yet how many there are. But one thing I know, it is me they are after—and there is very little love in their hearts. Wait . . ."

He concentrated on the single emotion pattern, trying to separate out this individual from all of the others. Putting to use all of the skills that he had been perfecting ever since the day he had discovered that he was an empathetic. He willed himself into the other's skin. Yes, the identity was positive. Brion nodded into the darkness.

"One mystery solved. Vjer is among them. At least we know now that he's not living alone out there in the hills. There must be a fair-sized population at home because he is bringing a good number of them with him to look for me."

"I thought you said he was your friend," Lea whispered.

"I thought so too. But that seems to have all changed. I'd like to know why—and I have a feeling that we are going to find out soon enough." He rose quietly and loosened the large knife in its sheath. "You just stay here out of sight while I sort them out."

"No!" Her fingers bit hard into his arm. "You can't go out there alone, in the darkness . . ."

"I certainly can. Please believe me when I say that I know what I'm doing." He took her hand gently away. "I need plenty of space around me when I meet them. And I don't want to have to worry about you at the same time. It's going to be all right."

Then he slipped away into the half-lit darkness. Staying flat on the ground and moving silently in the direction of the night stalkers. Stopping when he was well clear of Lea's hiding place. The emotions that he had been feeling were stronger now. There were at least a dozen individuals out there. Perhaps more. He waited until he could see their dark forms—there appeared to be about twenty of them—before he jumped to his feet and shouted.

"Vjer! I am here. What do you want?"

He could feel their dismay washing over their other emotions, sudden fear replacing hatred at his unexpected appearence. They stopped—all except one—who ignored the burst of fear, letting it be carried away by the hatred that had swallowed all other sensation. This man was still moving forward, doing something.

A spear appeared out of the night and buried itself in the ground a yard from Brion's feet. The situation was growing dangerous. He could sense that the others were getting over the first shock, were feeling the same hatred well up again. They started forward, one after the other.

Brion moved back from their steady advance, retreating towards the lake, away from the spot where Lea was hidden. She would be safe. He was not concerned about his own safety, feeling sure that he could take care of himself if the men attacked him—particularly if they were all like Vjer. He could outrun them if he couldn't outfight them. But why were they doing this? He shouted again to draw their attention.

That was when Lea screamed—and he felt her explosive burst of panic at the same moment.

Brion hurled himself in her direction. There was a man, two men, rising up before him—but he hit them at top speed, brushing them aside like insects, not even slowing. Lea screamed again and he could see the people who were holding her, the upraised spears. He never even thought of his knife as he crashed into them; his fists were weapons enough.

It was a wild melee in the star-touched darkness. They were so close that weapons were useless, even

a danger to those who wielded them. Hoarse cries of pain sounded as Brion picked up one of the men and hurled him into the largest group of attackers. His fists crushing down the three who had seized Lea. He thrust her behind him for protection, taking the frenzied blows of the spear hafts on his upraised arms. Striking back with fists more dangerous than clubs. The attackers fell back away from him—and the first of the stones crashed into the side of his head.

Brion roared in pain as more stones hit him, aware for the first time of the women who had been following behind the spear-armed attackers. Their weapons were rounded stones and they were deadly accurate with them. Brion seized up one of the spearmen to use his body as a shield—but too late. There were sharp blows on his neck and skull, impacts he never felt as he swayed, unconscious, toppling to the ground like a fallen tree. His last memory was of Lea's horrified screams and his inability to struggle to her through the enveloping blackness.

After that. Confusion. Mixed awareness. Blackness, redshot with pain. Swinging back and forth, pain in his wrists, his hand, his head. Motion. Blackness again. Once the stars were visible, swaying unsteadily before his eyes. He called out hoarsely to Lea. Did she answer? He could not remember. Pain and oblivion were his only reward.

The darkness had drained from the sky, and it was gray dawn before any measure of rational consciousness returned. He became aware of Lea's voice calling to him as he fought to open his crusted eyes. His arms and legs were immobilized somehow; he blinked until the blurs resolved themselves.

Leather thongs secured his ankles and wrists to a long pole; they were tied in place with strips of rawhide. His right hand was soaked with blood, throbbing with pain. He stretched it out so he could look at it and grunted with annoyance. Lea's whispered words were hoarse with worry.

"Are you alive? Can you hear me? Brion, please, can you hear me? Can you move?"

An inadvertant gasp of pain escaped his lips as he fought to move his head. His skull was bruised all over and one eye would not open all the way. The good one cleared enough so that he could make out Lea lying a few feet from him, bound as securely as he was to a second pole. At first he could only cough when he tried to talk, but he managed to force out the words.

"I'm all . . . right . . . fine."

"Fine!" There were tears in her voice, behind the anger. "You look absolutely terrible, all kicked about and bloody. If your head wasn't solid bone you would be dead by now . . . oh, Brion. It was terrible. They slung us from poles like corpses. Carried us all night. I was sure they had murdered you."

He tried to smile but could only grimace. "The reports of my death are greatly exaggerated." He moved his arms and legs as best he could against the restraints. "I feel bruised—but I don't think anything is broken. What about you?"

"Nothing important, a few scratches. You were the one they were hammering on. It was vicious, cruel . . ."

"Don't think about it now. We're alive and that is really all that counts for the moment. Now tell me everything that you saw on the way here."

"Little enough. We're in the hills somewhere. In a clearing in front of what appears to be some kind of natural caves in a cliff. There are tall trees all around the clearing. The women went into the cave when we arrived, they're still there. But the men are sleeping all around us."

"How many? Any of them awake or on guard?"

"I can count eighteen . . . no nineteen . . . twenty of them. I think's that all there are. If there's a guard posted I can't see him. Every once in awhile one of them will wake up and go off into the woods, their version of sanitary facilities I imagine."

"Sounds good. Just as indisciplined as I imagined. Right now is the best chance to get away, while they are asleep, before they do anything worse to us."

"Get away!" She shook her tightly bound wrists in his direction. "You've been hit on the head once too often. They've taken that big knife of yours, we can't reach these thongs with our teeth. So how do we do it?"

"I'll be just a moment," he said calmly. He closed his eyes and began taking deep and regular breaths.

It was important to order his thoughts, to concentrate all of his attention and energies. He had used these same breathing exercises when he was weight lifting; this effort now would be about the same. His body relaxed and he became aware of the myriad cuts and bruises. They were not important; as he narrowed his concentration they faded, unsensed. Good. Now he could feel his strength being focused, channeled. His eyes opened slowly and he looked down at the thick rawhide bindings about his wrists. The muscles in his arms and shoulders tensed.

Lea stared in astonishment. She saw him go limp, his muscles so under his command that even the flesh on his face grew slack. When his eyes opened they had a distant look, staring almost unseeingly at his wrists. A ripple of motion passed through his upper body and she could see his biceps swell as they tensed, pushing against his torn sleeves, widening the openings so that the weakened fabric tore and split. The rawhide bindings took the strain, creaking as they stretched, further and further. It was almost inhuman. His face remained calm while his arms moved slowly apart with slow, machine-like precision.

There was a small snapping sound as one of the bindings parted, then another. His hands were free.

Only when Brion realized this and relaxed did the shudder of fatigue run through his body. He dropped back to the ground, eyes shut and breathing hoarsely, rubbing his fingers over the deep welts in his wrists; coming away bloody where the flesh had been sliced to the bone by the rawhide. This lasted only a moment as he fought to regain control. Then he raised his head slowly and looked around.

"Very good," he said quietly. "As you said, all of them asleep."

With snake-like motions he slid over the hard-packed ground to her side, dragging with him the pole that was still attached to his ankles. He examined Lea's bindings.

"If you try to tear these off you'll tear my wrists off along with them," she said, trying not to look at the slow coursing of blood down his hands.

"Don't worry, yours will be a lot easier than mine." He bent forward and closed his teeth on the lizard skin bindings. Clamping down and chewing strongly. They parted in less than a minute. "Tastes terrible," he said, spitting out some fragments.

"You must have had a good dentist." There was a quaver behind the forced lightness of her words. He reached up and brushed a matted hank of hair from before her eyes.

"We'll be out of this soon, take my word for that. Just lie quiet for a moment more."

He was not as relaxed as he pretended to be. It was full daylight now and their movements could easily be seen by anyone who might be stirring. The next few minutes were vital. If they reached the trees before the alarm was given he knew they could get away. Bruised or not he would run—and they would not be captured a second time. He separated the strands of rawhide that bound his ankles, then inserted the index finger of his left hand under the thinnest of them. It broke easily. He snapped the rest, a single strand at a time, then stripped away the fragments and slowly sat up. His captors were still all asleep. He tore Lea's ankles free from the pole in the same way.

"Here we go," he whispered, scooping her up in his arms and rising, walking carefully among the silent bodies. Quickly and silently, waiting for the alarm to be raised, but still hearing nothing. Six, seven—eight paces and they were among the trees and pushing through the shrubbery.

"I'll be back in a moment," he said, placing her gently on the ground. His finger on her lips silenced her shocked response. Then he was gone, back into the clearing, and she did not know whether to laugh or to cry.

It was laughter. She could barely contain her
half-hysterical mirth when he reappeared carrying
one of their captors. Simply escaping wasn't enough
for him—oh, no. He had to take a prisoner as well!
The man struggled and kicked feebly, but to no
avail. Brion had captured him silently by simply
clutching the man's mouth with one great hand,
lifting him bodily from the ground at the same time.
The man was half-suffocated now, his eyes bulging
from his reddened face. When Brion released his
grip the prisoner sucked air into his lungs with a
single shuddering gasp. Before he could release the
breath and shout, a hard fist caught him below the
ear and he slumped unconscious to the ground.

Brion ignored him as he dropped, turning instead to Lea and helping her to her feet."

"Can you walk all right?" he asked.

"Stagger is more like it."

"Do your best. I'll help you if you need it."

He slung the captive over his shoulder with an easy motion, then took Lea by the arm and led the way through the trees and down the hillside. Getting farther and farther from the encampment with each passing moment.

There was no alarm. For the moment, at least, they were free.

NINE

Electronic Inquisition

Brion came to the edge of the forest and paused beneath the largest tree there. He looked down the grassy slope to the empty plain beyond, past it to the vast blue waters of the Central Lake that stretched away to the horizon. The day was warm now, with the sun high in the sky. Behind him he could hear Lea stumbling through the underbrush, almost falling, muttering a choked oath. He reached past her with his senses, outward to the limit of his ability, but could still find no trace of any pursuit.

"Is there any reason . . . we can't rest here . . . for a bit," she gasped, leaning against the tree at his side.

"Of course not. This is a good place to stop." She was slipping to the ground even as he spoke. "As far as I can tell no one is after us yet, so we're safe here for the moment. But once we are out on the plain we'll be easy to see. We must decide now what we want to do next."

"Why not drop graybeard for openers," Lea said, waving towards the limp body over Brion's shoulder. "Or have you forgotten you were carrying him?"

Brion let his burden slip down onto the matted leaves. "He's not heavy. Very thin and old as you can see."

"Is that the best one you could find?"

"Yes. He may represent some kind of authority, since he's the only one I observed who was wearing any kind of non-functional decoration." Brion moved aside the matted gray hair of the man's beard to reveal the necklace of bleached bones that he wore about his neck. "He might have answers to questions that the others might not know."

"Do you mean you actually took the time to look around and pick and choose when you went back to grab a prisoner?"

"Of course. It was a unique opportunity."

"Some day I'm going to understand you—but not today. I'm thirsty and hungry and exhausted, and feel as though someone has walked all over me with spiked shoes. Have you given any thought to our future?"

"A very great deal. There was both the time and the opportunity for concentration while we were walking. First, we must face some unpleasant facts. All of the equipment we were carrying is missing, as well as our food and water, my knife . . ."

"And if that radio controller isn't still hidden in that crater where you put it, we might as well sign a mutual suicide pact right now. I don't look forward to those types laying their hands on me a second time . . . '' She leaned forward to look closely at their prisoner; then wrinkled her nose with disgust. ''How awful. Since we're speaking of hands—aren't those human finger bones strung on Dirty's necklace?''

Brion nodded. ''I found that fact most interesting. That's why I brought him. I also have a strong personal interest in that necklace.''

There was an edge of anger in his voice that had not been there before, that made her look at the necklace again. Bleached finger bones, one of them darker than the others. No, not darker, different. She looked more closely and saw that it was a freshly severed finger, the blood still caked darkly

upon it. With sudden realization she stared, horrified, at Brion. He nodded grimly. Holding up his right hand so that all four of his remaining fingers could be clearly seen. Lea gasped.

"They did that to you—they're filth! You didn't let me know . . ."

"No point in doing that since there's nothing either of us can do about it now. It's not too serious, they tied a thong around the stump to stop the bleeding. But I am most curious about the significance of the act. This man will be able to tell us." He dismissed the matter with a wave of his truncated hand. "But that is all in the future. Before we do anything else we must call the lifeship down. And I hope that you are correct about our radio controller, that it remains untouched. Until we get to it we have no way of knowing. Then we must reach the crater as soon as possible and signal the lifeship to land. You will board it and leave at once . . ."

"Without you? Do you really like this disgusting place so much?"

"Not particularly. But the work we have to do must be done here. And I don't want this man in the ship."

"Why? Afraid he'll take it over?"

"Quite the opposite. I have an informed hunch, backed up by the feelings I sensed in Vjer, that it would be disaster to take any of these people out of their natural environment. I'll be perfectly safe remaining here until you return. While the lifeship is completing a single orbit you will have time enough to assemble the items from a list that we will prepare now. After the orbit you can land with what we will need."

"Shouldn't I make a recording of what we have discovered so far?"

"That is item one on your list. After you do that you must get together the equipment that we will need. It is unavoidable that a number of items will have a high metallic content. I believe that it is still very important not to have any metal on our persons when we move about. But if I find that the fragment of wing is still undisturbed, why then we will know that we have a cache where we could leave these metal items until we need them."

"Items such as a few stun grenades, a gun or two?"

"Very much what I had in mind. I have no desire for a rerun of last night's performance."

"A hearty second to that motion." She climbed wearily to her feet. "I'm ready to go if you are. I get a very itchy feeling sitting here with my back to these woods."

"You must be tested to see if you have empathetic powers," Brion said, slowly hoisting the still-unconscious man to his shoulder. "They are out there now looking for us, I have been aware of it for some minutes. But I sense only worry and confusion so I don't think they have found our trail."

"Now you tell me! Let's move." She scrambled to her feet and started down the hill.

Brion broke into an easy jog so that he caught up and passed her within a few paces. "I'm going ahead," he told her. "They'll probably be able to see us once we are out on the plain, so I want to send for the lifeship as soon as possible."

"Don't stand there talking—move it out! I'm right behind you."

She was running as fast as she could, but still

could not match his speed. Brion loped out ahead of
her in ground-eating strides, his course taking him
directly to the crater. Lea kept looking over her
shoulder as she ran, then she had to walk for a bit to
catch her breath, before she was able to run again.
She struggled her way up a small rise and when she
reached the top she saw Brion, far ahead, climbing
out of the crater—waving something that glinted in
the sun. The controller was still there!

"The lifeship, it's on the way down," he said as she
stumbled up to him. "And there is no sign of any
pursuers as yet."

"I've never been . . . so tired in my life." She
gasped out the words as she dropped to the ground.
Brion put the controller at her side and started back
towards the crater.

"Give me a shout if he starts to move," he said. "I
want to make another copy of the identification
plate I found on the wrecked wing. The first one is
gone, I had it scratched onto my waterbottle. When
you are in the ship use the modem to put this copy
into the record." He slipped over the edge.

Lea looked at the necklace around the snoring
man's neck and shuddered. What animals these
people were. Cutting a man's finger off just like that.
For what reason? It must have been an important
reason for them, with a ritual meaning or something. And Brion's hand, how it must have hurt, yet
he had never mentioned it. He was an unbelievable
man in every way. But the stump would have to be
treated at once to prevent infection; a medkit must
be high on their list of necessities. A new finger
would be regrown eventually—but that was not
going to stop the pain and discomfort now.

"I've copied the symbols as best I could, onto this piece of bark," Brion said, when he had clambered back out of the crater. "Can you make any sense of them at all?"

She turned the bark around and around, then shook her head *no*. "It's not any language that I am acquainted with. Though the alphabet has a familiar look. The memory banks may come up with something . . ."

Their gray-haired prisoner opened his eyes and began to tremble and scream hoarsely, scrabbling to crawl away from them. Brion reached out and seized him, then pressed his thumb hard against the side of the man's neck below the ear. The prisoner flopped twice and was still.

"Did you see that?" Brion asked.

"The way you crunched him unconscious? I sure did. You'll have to teach me that trick . . ."

"No, not that. What he was looking at when he started to wail. It was the radio controller."

"Could he have known what it is?"

"I doubt that very much. But it must have some terrible significance for him that we will have to determine." Brion turned his head sideways, listening. "The ship is on the way down. You must memorize the list now, of the things that we will need."

The lifeship was on the ground for less than two minutes. Brion worried for every second of the time. Even when the ship had lifted off again with Lea aboard, the nagging concern continued. It had landed safely twice—which indicated that this location might not be under continuous observation. But each time it came down the danger of possible discovery increased. Yet they had to stay in this area because the hunters were the only key they had to the deadly problem of this planet. Since there was no choice he forced himself to put the danger from his mind and concentrate on setting up the HLP.

The small metal case of the Heuristic Language Programmer contained a wealth of sophisticated circuitry and design. It functioned through a holographic projector that formed a three-dimensional image—an image that apparently floated in the air above it. The first image that appeared was a tilted white surface with operating instructions printed upon it. Brion read this and punched into the controls the codes that he wanted. The instructions vanished and the teacher-image appeared in their place. This was an elderly man dressed in a plain gray outfit who sat, crosslegged, with a lidless box on the ground before him. Brion worked with the controls until he had replaced the man's suit with a loincloth affair, and had managed to lengthen the image's hair as well. Though their prisoner was much filthier, teacher and student resembled each other very much.

Brion looked at the frozen three-dimensional image and nodded. It was good enough. A touch of a final control caused the image to move backward in space so that it concealed the projection mechanism. When this happened it looked as though Brion's arm had been plunged deep into the man's naked thigh. He withdrew his hand, satisfied.

As soon as the task was completed the worry returned. Nor would it recede until the lifeship had landed and taken off safely again with Lea aboard. Now all he had to worry about were the remaining members of the tribe. There was no sign of them yet, nor could he detect their presence anywhere nearby. The seconds ticked slowly by.

Nothing had changed by the time the ship had returned and landed. He stood and waved. "Just drop the equipment down to me, one item at a time," he called out to Lea when the airlock had opened. "Then get down yourself as fast as you can."

It was dangerous—but it was the fastest way to get the equipment unloaded. He caught the heavy containers, one after another, stacking them to one side, then hurrying them into the crater as Lea climbed down to join him. As soon as they were clear of the blast area of the ship he punched in the commands that sent it back into orbit again. Only after it was gone and there had been no retaliation from the sky could they relax. Lea shook her fist at the distant hills.

"All right out there, you can come back now, come down here and try to cause some more trouble. Are you going to get a lovely surprise this time! It will be my pleasure. Not one of you smelly creatures is worth a finger of Brion's hand!"

"I appreciate the sentiments," he said, putting a bandage over the antiseptic foam that had been spread on the stump of the missing finger. He looked down. "Our guest seems to be stirring again."

"I'll go get us some food while you start up the machine. You can find out if it's possible to strike up a conversation with him."

The education technique of the HLP was painfully slow and painstakingly precise. It was essential that the subject cooperate at all times. This proved difficult because there was no active cooperation by the captive at first, something that was necessary to make this technique work. It wasn't that the man was belligerent—just that he was terrified out of his wits.

Brion had known that the man was about to awake when he sensed the unconscious brain rhythms begin to change. First there was worry and a sensation of pain, and nothing else until he opened his eyes. Then they were replaced by simple and unmitigated fear, the same fear that had possessed Vjer when he had first seen Brion. But this was worse because it was unending and relentless. When the captive focused his eyes on Brion he tried to scramble away, mewling with terror. Brion seized him by the ankle to prevent his escape, but when he did this the sensation of fear grew even stronger. The man moaned in agony, venting his bowels uncontrollably. His eyes rolled up so that only the whites showed as he fainted. Brion went to get the medkit.

"Would you like some food?" Lea asked as he joined her in the shelter of the crater.

"Not quite yet. He's being very uncooperative, so I'm going to give him the shot of scopalamine that the instructions recommended for this kind of case."

The slight sting of the subcutaneous pressure spray from the capsule stirred the man to consciousness; Brion slipped the device into his pocket before it could be seen. This time a numbness spread over the captive's fear. The man moved uncomfortably, wiping at himself, eyeing Brion with fear-ridden suspicion. Brion did nothing, simply sat on the ground and waited. He could see the man looking at the projected image, and at the same time felt the first touches of curiosity behind the ebbing fear. To the prisoner's eyes the image was that of a man of his own age. A man who appeared to have astonishing body control, for he sat, not moving his body in the slightest, just breathing very lightly. Without this computer simulation of life the image would have been a statue. When the curiosity grew stronger Brion spoke the cueword softly.

"Begin."

The captive glanced at Brion with a sudden spurt of fear—then back to the image which had stirred for the first time. The image nodded and smiled, then reached into the open box that was sitting on the ground before him. He withdrew his hand holding what appeared to be an ordinary rock.

"Rock," the image said clearly. "Rock . . . rock." Each time it spoke the word it nodded and smiled. Then it extended the rock and made an interrogative sound. The old man only gaped, his brain filled with confusion.

With infinite machine patience the image repeated the demonstration and the interrogative. There was no positive reaction. On the third repetition the image was no longer smiling. When the old man did not answer to its interrogation the face grew ugly, the lips drew back from the teeth, it frowned—expressing every outward indication of aggression and anger that the anthropologists had ever discovered in any culture. The captive quailed away, moaning with fear. On the next repetition, when the rock was thrust in his direction, he stammered out *Prtr*. The image smiled and nodded and made all kinds of reinforcing friendly gestures. The learning process had begun.

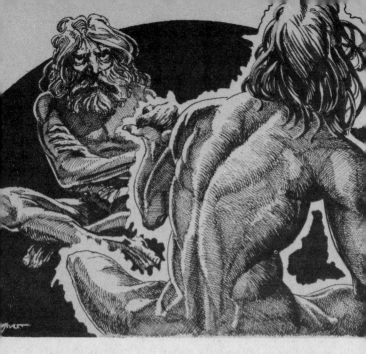

Brion had moved back out of the old man's line of vision, so his presence would not interrupt the lesson. He watched as the image poured water, over and over again, from one container to another, never spilling a drop.

"Does this really work?" Lea asked.

"Every time. The computer program is self-checking. As soon as a few words are memorized it will play them back to the subject for cross reference. As its vocabulary grows the process is speeded up. Within a short period of time it will be able to ask questions, simple ones at first, then more and more abstract ones. When the old man gets tired, the machine will give him time to rest. Then it can teach us whatever it has learned."

"Drilling us and correcting our accents, grammar and all the rest I suppose?"

"Exactly. Now where's that food you were talking about? I don't have to watch the man to keep track of him. His emotional patterns will let me know if he is up to anything.

It was late afternoon before the captive began to nod with fatigue. Brion brought him some water in a wooden bowl and he slurped at it noisily.

"What's his name?" Brion asked the HLP.

"The subject is named Ravn. Ravn. Ravn. I repeat, Ravn . . . "

"That's enough." He turned and smiled broadly. "Ravn: Welcome to the human race."

TEN

Taking Charge

"The wound is healing quite well," Lea said, holding Brion's hand and turning it back and forth as she looked at the stump of the missing finger. She spread antiseptic cream on the wound while he watched.

"*Arb't klrm*," he said.

"If you are trying to say 'That hurt', you've got to learn to swallow the terminal sounds a good deal more, or the noisome natives are never going to understand you."

"It's a pretty repulsive language."

"That's just your linguistic isolationism talking, Brion. Taken abstractly, no language can possibly be repulsive . . ."

Brion interrupted her with a raised finger, then spoke quietly. "Don't look now, but Ravn is trying to

125

make a run for it. I've been waiting for this. I'll give
him a bit of a lead before I grab him. I want him to
run and to feel that he is getting away from us at last.
Then, when I grab him again, he should be in despair. Perhaps I can get through to him then when
his defense are down, convince him to talk to me. I
haven't wanted to force it up until now. But if he has
this much energy I think that he can use some shaking up."

"Give him an extra shake for me. Whenever he
looks at me he has that same disgusted expression
that he had when you gave him the cooked meat to
eat."

"His is a very stratified society, you saw that for
yourself."

"Yes. With women somewhere below the bottom.
Ahh, there he goes. He's getting to his feet now,
looking in this direction."

"Turn away as though you don't see him. I want
him to have some hope of escape—before I take it
away from him. This should be a traumatic situation that might very well get him off his guard."

Ravn knew that the Old One Who Talked would
not pursue him. He sat always in the same place.
And of course the She was of no importance. It was
only the big Hunter he feared, for this one's strength
was like that of two men. Yet the chance must be
taken now, when the Hunter was not looking. Ravn
had eaten and rested. He was the Ravn and still
strong in the legs since for many years he had pur-
sued and killed Meat-things. He had outrun
them—and now he would outrun the Hunter as well.
The Hunter was stupid, not even looking. The Old
One was stupid too for he just sat there and gave no
alarm. Slowly at first, this was the way, he crept

away through the grass—now leap up, fast! Like the wind, like the Meat-things—he would never be caught now.

Lea watched the old man running fleetly across the plain, further and further away. "Aren't you taking a risk?" she asked. "The old bastard has a good turn of speed. It would be a shame to lose him now. There could be trouble, you might have to fight with his friends. They could be waiting for him out there."

"Please don't be concerned. There's no one waiting, I'm sure of that." Brion looked after the fleeing man, then stood and stretched. "Sprinting is good exercise. I don't get enough of it."

As she watched him, Lea knew that she has been foolish to worry. When Brion began to run she realized that she had never seen him move at top speed before. She had forgotten that he was a world champion athlete, a victor in twenty sports—and this had to have been one of them.

For Ravn it was an unwelcome shock. One instant he had been ready to sing a victory song, having run so far and so fast that he knew that he could never be caught. When he looked back and saw the Hunter beginning to chase him he laughed, going faster himself in order to open the distance. But when he looked again the Hunter had halved the distance—and was still coming on. Ravn wailed in despair and ran, but he could not escape. Heavy footsteps pounded close behind him while the trees were still too distant. His lungs ached, his heart was bursting—a heavy hand fell onto his shoulder and he shrieked aloud and fell.

Brion felt no pity as he looked down at the old man writhing and wailing in the grass. He felt his heart

beating strongly after the run, and with each pulsa-
tion the stump of his amputated finger throbbed
with pain. An uncomfortable reminder that this
groveling creature was the very one who had amputated it. Anger cut through Brion's pain as he saw
that same finger around the filthy creature's neck,
saw the man clutch to the necklace of bones with
both hands as he lay there screeching with self pity.
Holding on to it as if it gave him strength.

When he saw this, Brion knew what he had to do.
He remembered that the ragged lizard skin clothing
and crude stone weapons were the only artifacts
that these people appeared to have. Other than this
necklace. It *must* be valued highly, or was some kind
of honor to wear. Good! In that case he was the one
who was going to have it.

Ravn wailed even louder when Brion tried to take
the necklace from him, clutching to it desperately
with both hands. But Brion's strength could not be
resisted. He seized Ravn's wrists with his mighty
hands and squeezed, numbing them instantly so
that the fingers lost their strength and simply fell
open. Brion pulled the necklace off over Ravn's
head, then put it slowly on himself. The old man's
wailings gave way to screamed entreaty.

"Mine—give me! I am the Ravn, mine to wear,
mine . . ."

He spoke in his own language and Brion found
that he could understand it easily enough. The
Heuristic Language Programmer had done its work
well. Brion stepped back and placed his hand on the
necklace, speaking slowly in the same language.

"It is mine now. I am Brion. While I wear it I am
the Ravn." If Ravn were a title as well as a name this
should make sense to the man. And it did. The

screaming stopped and Ravn's eyes narrowed with anger.

"Only one Ravn with the people. Me. Mine." He extended his hand with a demanding gesture. Brion took the necklace off again but did not release it.

"Is this yours?" he asked.

"Mine. Give me. Belongs to the Ravn."

"What is a Ravn:"

"I am. I tell you to give it. You are rotten meat, you are shit, you are woman . . ."

Brion casually took the old man's neck in one hand and tightened his grip, pulling the man up towards him at the same time, until their faces almost touched. He growled as he spoke.

"You curse me. You do not curse Brion. Who could Kill you in an instant by making tighter his fingers—like this."

Ravn's body flapped about in agony; he could not breathe or talk and death was very close.

Brion shook him about like a rag, then waved the necklace of bones before his face. "You will tell me what I want to know. Then you will have this back. You understand me? Say yes. *Say yes!*"

"Yes . . ." Ravn gasped. "Yes."

Brion did not let the sensation of victory show in his face. The anger was still in his voice when he dropped Ravn to the ground and sat beside him. His questions were imperative and demanded an answer. Ravn answered them, as best he could, concealing nothing. After a great amount of time had passed his voice became hoarse and his words stumbled one over the other. It was more than enough for a beginning, Brion thought. He was about to return the necklace when he noticed his own amputated finger threaded into place among the bones. It was a part of him—and it must have had some important meaning to these people or they would not have taken it in this manner. Well they weren't going to get it back. Brion seized the dry flesh of the thing and tore it from the necklace.

"This is mine forever. The rest you can have for now." Brion hurled the necklace to the ground. "We will now go back to my place. You will talk to me again whenever I wish it."

Ravn slipped the necklace over his head with trembling hands, then pushed himself to his feet. All rebellion had vanished. Brion knew that from now on the old man would do everything that he was told. As soon as the other's back was turned Brion let the dessicated finger slip to the ground, happy to be rid of the thing. It had served its purpose.

"Woman, we will eat!" Brion called out in the native language as he led his exhausted prisoner back to their camp. Lea flared her nostrils at his words and tone of voice.

"Does this male chauvenist pig act mean that we are finally getting somewhere with Old Dirty here?"

"It does, my precious one." He winked as he shouted the words. "Please feed him, then I can put him to bed, after which I will tell you some of the interesting things I have learned."

"If you don't mind, we'll eat separately. I never have got used to his diet of decayed raw meat."

"I've found out about that as well. Let's feed him and stake him out. I don't think he'll give us any more trouble."

Ravn's loud snores sounded from the high grass where he had been bedded down for the night—with a braided length of rawhide securing his foot to a stake driven deep into the ground. He would be there when they wanted him.

"They're primitives," Brion said, chewing steadily on the dried rations. "Unbelievably primitive in every way, with all of their activities determined by strict taboos. Men are hunters and in control of all activities . . ."

"Not for the first time in the history of mankind."

"Agreed. But this an all or nothing society, completely black and white without any shades of gray that I can find so far. The men hunt, and everyone eats what they bring back. Raw, as we know. Eating anything else is taboo. Eating cooked food is taboo. Leaving the forest for the plain is taboo—other than brief forays for hunting. Men may make and use weapons, but anyone else . . ."

"I know. It's taboo. Did you find out why they staged that night attack when they captured us?"

"Still the taboo thing. They saw us near the lifeship—and machines appear to be the biggest taboo of all."

"That might have something to do with the war machines."

"I'm sure it does, but that's all I could get out of him at the time."

"Did you at least discover what was so important about the bone necklace."

"I think I did. It's complicated and I didn't follow some of the words, but it seems to work like this. A man has a spirit, some sort of essential being. Women and children don't, as you might have guessed. They just die and are forgotten like animals. But if a piece of a man is kept by the Ravn, why then he is considered still alive and part of the tribe, and still subject to the Ravn's discipline. They were going to kill us in some ritually delightful way because we are taboo. But he was keeping my finger because that way I would always be under his control."

"Delightful. Does this mean that stashed away someplace they have the finger bones of all their ancestors?"

"Probably. But essentially this sort of logic is no different in principal from all of the other cultures that bury their dead. In fact this is more practical. Just keeping a finger bone is a lot easiesr than a complete skeleton."

Lea looked up at the star-filled sky and shivered.

"And these people are descendants of cultured and intelligent human beings. How did this ever happen?"

"I have no idea. Yet."

"What is the connection between these primitives and the modern warfare we have seen here?"

"I have no idea of the answer to that one either. But I intend to find out. If Ravn doesn't know, or pretends not to know, then some of the others will tell me. And they may have artifacts that will give us a clue. So this all comes down to the inescapable fact that we will just have to go up into the hills and see them. Find out for ourselves. They have been on this planet for thousands of years, probably since before the Breakup. They must be able to tell us something."

"You keep saying *us*. Are you trying to tell me that you intend to risk our necks back at their campsite again?"

"The risk will be minimal this time." He pointed to the case of weapons. "We go armed and we go by choice."

ELEVEN

Trek Into Danger

Slowly, in single file, they trudged across the plain towards the forested hills beyond. Ravn led the way with Brion following closely behind him. Lea stumbled along far in the rear, heavily burdened by the skin-wrapped bundle on her back. She wiped the perspiration from her face with her forearm and called out.

"Hold it right there! It's well past time for a break."

She threw the bundle to the ground when she had caught up with Brion, then dropped down on it with a grateful sigh.

"Drink some water," Brion said. "Take a rest."

"How nice of you to offer!" She spat out the words. "Generous too, to let me drink some of the water that I have been carrying on my back all day."

"But we have no other choice, do we?" he said,

135

speaking with the voice of sweet logic. She wasn't buying it.

"What does that *we* stuff mean—when I'm the one doing the carrying. I know that the argument is foolproof, that women do all the heavy work, like beasts of burden, in this broken-down society, that you would sacrifice all your prestige if you carried anything. Meanwhile I'm sacrificing my spinal column and will undoubtedly develop terminal hernia—don't smile at me in that condescending manner, you filthy brute!"

"Sorry. I wish I could help. But we should be there soon."

"Not soon enough . . ."

She opened the pungent lizard skin wrappings—the creature had reluctantly become dinner for Ravn just two days earlier—and rooted about until she found the water bottle. She drank deeply, then passed it to Brion. He just used it to wet his lips. Since she had drunk from it the water was taboo for a Hunter; they made no attempt to even offer it to Ravn.

"When you put the water away, hand me the case of percussion grenades," Brion said it too casually. She looked up, startled.

"Is there trouble coming?" she asked. He nodded slowly.

"They must be under cover in the forest. I can feel their hatred, the same as last time."

"But not quite the same as last time!" She passed him the flat box and nodded encouragingly as he slipped a handful of the metal spheres into his pocket. "You don't know how much I'm looking forward to this."

"We don't want to injure any of them. But it will
be most effective to throw a large fright into them. If
we can establish ourselves on top of the social structure, they should answer any questions that we
might ask. We'll move now, but stay near me because they are sure to close in behind us. They're
good hunters and they are armed, so we don't want
to take any chances."

If Ravn was aware of the prepared ambush he
gave no sign, just trudged on ahead of them at the
same steady pace. They wended their way through
the shrubs, then on among the taller trees. A large
clearing opened up before them. Their path lay
across it.

"Stop here," Brion called out in the native tongue
when they were halfway across. "Give me water to
drink," he ordered Lea. Then added more quietly;
"They are on all sides of us now and they are very
tense. I'm sure that they'll attack any moment now.
Keep your hand in the bundle and near the guns, just
in case . . ."

The silence of the forest was shattered by a high-
pitched, warbling cry that echoed across the glade.
It was instantly joined by the massed war-cries of
the Hunters as they erupted on all sides. Ravn
started forward to join them—but Brion was on him
in an instant; a single blow of his fist against the
man's shoulder sending him crashing to the ground.
Brion placed one foot on his back to hold him there,
then began to throw the grenades towards the en-
circling trees, one hurtling after the other.

Flame and sound exploded on all sides. Lea had
known what was coming and had covered her ears;
nevertheless she still fell to her knees, quivering

under the impact of the brain-shattering sound. The battle cries turned to howls of pain as the men fell back or collapsed. In the silence that followed Brion's voice roared out with anger, cursing them in their own language.

"You are dirt. You are women. You are shit! You raise a spear towards me and I kill you. You are dead meat under my foot—like this Ravn who is dead meat." He leaned some of his massive weight onto the man as he talked and the Ravn wailed impressively. Brion had the upper hand and he meant to keep it. He sensed nothing except unreasoning fear from all of the Hunters. One of the sensation patterns was more familiar than the others.

"Vjer—come here," he ordered.

The Hunter rose hesitantly to his feet and stumbled forward. There was blood running from his nose, and he was dazed, numbed by the explosions. Brion fixed him with a glare.

"Who am I?" he called out.

"You are Brrn . . ."

"Louder, I cannot hear you."

"BRRN."

"What is this piece of dirt I stand upon?"

"That is the Ravn."

"Then who am I now?"

"You must be . . . the Ravn Above Ravn!" His eyes were wide as he spoke and Brion could sense the awe, the almost worshipful quality of his emotions. Brion pointed to the plasteel knife that Vjer was holding.

"What is that in your hand?"

Vjer looked at the knife and began to shake. He dropped to his knees with fear and crawled forward

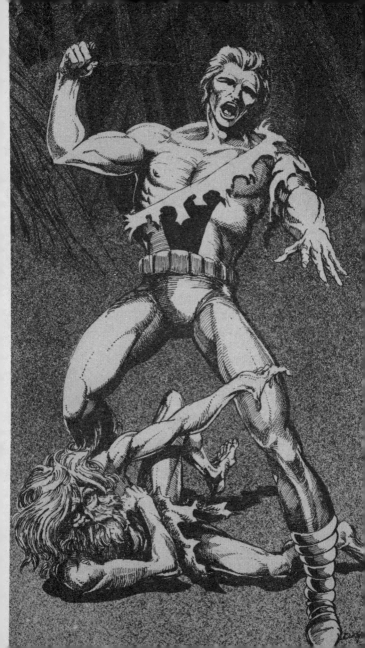

to lay it at Brion's feet. Brion picked it up and slipped it back into his empty sheath.

"Now we will go on," he said, taking his foot from the Ravn's back. The title he had been given was of greatest importance; he could sense that by the reactions of the men around him. The aggression and fear were fading as he was accepted in his new role.

"They still have their weapons," Lea said, eyeing the Hunters with suspicion.

"There is no need to disarm them, since I am now a part of their culture in this new role."

"And what about me? I know, a woman, less than nothing. Carry the bundle and shut up. But wait until I have you out of this male-chauvenistic paradise, Brion Brandd! Oh, how you are going to pay for this . . ."

As they climbed the hillside through the trees, Brion kept his senses aware of the men about him. As long as they accepted him he was safe. But this could change in an instant, for reasons he might not even be aware of. But if this new-found status continued to work this would be the quickest and most successful way to penetrate the culture and talk to the people. It was dangerous. But it was too late to turn back.

Once the aggression and hatred had been removed, with no reason to stay together, the Hunters began to drift away one at a time. Only a handful stayed with them all the way to the settlement. They worked their way up a steep hill, until a rocky cliff was visible ahead through the trees. It slanted back to form a string of natural caves. A small group of women were working here, scraping the flesh from lizard skins with bits of sharp stone. They retreated when they saw the strangers, being speeded along with kicks and blows from a gray-haired woman.

"Must be a female version of Ravn," Lea said, looking on with interest. "Since you seem to have established yourself as top dog with the Hunters, I'm going to do the same with the ladies." She dropped the bundle and followed the women towards the cave, calling out for them to stop. They only ran the faster, all except the gray haired woman. She wheeled about and rushed at Lea.

"I kill! You dirt," she screeched.

Lea settled her weight evenly on both feet and drew back a small, hard fist. As her adversary ran up she swung a punch with all of her strength right into the pit of the woman's stomach. She folded nicely, wailing with pain, her arms clutched about her midriff. Lea seized her by the hair and dragged her face around.

"Shut up and tell me your name—or I'll hit you again."

"I am . . . First Woman."

"No more. I am First Woman. You are now Old Woman."

The newly named Old Woman wailed again in protest, at the same time trying to pry Lea's fingers from her hair. The wail turned to a scream of pain as Ravn passed by and casually kicked her in the side.

"You are now Old Woman," he said, happy to see some one else humiliated as he had been. He went on to seat himself against the rock wall, in the sun, then screamed for food.

"Charming people," Lea said.

"Products of their culture," Brion answered,

wrapping a piece of lizard skin around the communicator before he took it from the bundle. "And the system obviously works for survival on this planet—or these people would not be here. I'm going to have the lifeship's computer enter a report into its memory about what happened today. We want to keep the record complete and up to date, just in case something happens to us . . ."

"Don't depress me any more, if you please. I believe that we are going to finish this assignment—alive. Keep that idea firmly in your skull. While you're doing that I'm going to talk to the women. See what this repulsive world looks like from their point of view."

"Good. We need information, but we don't want to stay here any longer than we have to. Most of them have vermin, have you noticed that?"

"Hard to miss. I get itchy just looking at them. Don't go too far away."

"I'll be right here. I want to do some questioning myself. I'll talk to Vjer since I have already established a relationship there. Good luck."

It was almost dark before Lea emerged from the cave, scratching grimly under her arm. Brion was talking to two of the Hunters, but he sent them away when he saw her expression. He held up a plastic container. "I found some antiseptic spray in the medkit that will make a good insectiside."

"Use it, please! That cave is literally a pesthole."

She quickly stripped off her clothes and sprayed her body, which was covered with red welts. Brion then used the spray on her clothing while she rubbed healing cream into her skin. She called out to him as she was dressing again.

"Be an angel and pour me a large double vodka. The flask is down at the bottom of the bundle."

"I'll join you. It's been a long day for both of us. How did your question session go?"

"Fine, if you don't consider the bug bites. Right to the top, that's right, thanks. My, that feels delicious going down. The women have a sub-culture of their own, arranged strictly by rank, and a wonderful trove of stories as well. There appears to be a myth or a mnemonic chant for everything you could possibly name. It's a complete oral history. I'll take a recorder next time. This will be priceless material for the anthropologists. Now tell me what you found out."

"Very little. The Hunters talked to me easily enough, but only about killing this animal or the other, or about their own great prowess in the chase. You can well imagine the sort of thing. Other than these topics they have no personal opinions. They are just walking collections of taboos. Everything they do or think is governed by this system."

"It's the same with the women, at least in their physical life. But they escape into myth very easily, and that activity seems to be totally outside the taboo areas. Though I have a feeling that the stories are probably taboo for men. Did you hear anything about the creation myth?"

Brion shook his head. "No, nothing like that."

"It's interesting because it might very well be a simplified version of a true history, something that is still remembered, but only in mythical form. The story says that at one time the people lived like gods, that they moved over the ground without using their feet, and even flew through the air without having wings like the flying lizards. In those time the people

were wrong because they treasured many things
that were made of *ckl't*—have you run across the
word?"

"Yes, and I know what it is. Metal. From the way
the word was used I suspected what it meant, but I
had to lose one of my subjects to find out that my
theory was right. I made him look at the transceiver
and the mere sight of it turned him into a bundle of
blind fear. He actually ran headlong into a tree as he
was trying to get away from the thing."

"Better and better. The historical myth goes like
this. The ancient people who treasured metal
thought themselves gods, therefore the true gods
destroyed them and their metal, and the metal
places where they lived. Then the gods made them
go out and live like the animals until they became
purified. So if the people continue to live in this
manner they will be pure again and will be admitted
to a *chl't*, I translated the word as paradise which is
probably right. Meanwhile people must suffer in
this world, obeying all of the taboos that enable
them to live in the proper manner so that one day
they will be able to enter paradise."

"That's tremendous!" Brion said, jumping to his
feet and pacing back and forth, unable to sit still
with excitement. "You are amazing, you've done a
wonderful job. Every bit of what you say fits—if
these people are exactly what they appear to be.
Refugees from a global holocaust. They were invaded, or were defeated in war, and had to flee their
cities. They saw their armies and war machines
destroyed. So now they blame their destruction on
the gods. It's a lot easier to do that then admit
defeat."

"A fine theory, professor," Lea said, draining her

glass and smacking her lips. She poured herself another one. "There is just one small thing wrong with it that I can see. Where are the victorious and conquering armies now? All the evidence we have seen indicates that this war is still being fought."

"Yes," Brion said, sitting down glumly. "I hadn't thought of that. So now we really know little more than we did when we started."

"Don't despair. We know a lot. For one thing I explored our underground city theory, and all I got were empty stares. If the civilization on this world is underground these people don't know a thing about it."

"Which appears to be just about as much as we know. I'm beginning to think that we have hit a dead end."

"Well you may have, Ravn Above Ravn, with your Hunters and fighters and all that big machismo stuff." She hiccupped sweetly and touched the back of her hand to her mouth, smiling. "We girls had a more sensible conversation, as befits the more attractive and intelligent sex. As I am sure I told you, all metal is taboo, and machines made of metal are the most taboo of all—as we discovered out the hard way when they spotted us near a metal flying ship. So, therefore, doesn't it stand to reason that the most impossibly taboo place of all would be the place where the machines come from. Do you follow me so far?"

"Yes, of course. Do you really need another glass of vodka?"

"Shut up. Now wouldn't it be very nice if we knew where the machines came from?"

"Of course, but . . ."

"But me no buts. You see I know. They told me how to find this place. So all we have to do now is go there—and the mystery will be solved."

She admired his expression, all hanging jaw and staring eyes. Then she closed her own eyes and quietly went to sleep.

TWELVE

Discovery!

Brion had an almost overwhelming desire to shake Lea awake, to force her to give some explanation of just what she had been talking about. He resisted. It had been a long and exhausting day for her; she must have kept going on nerve alone. When he went to put the bottle of vodka away he saw that she had drunk only a small amount. It was fatigue, not drink, that had dropped her in her tracks. Although the night was warm, as always, he spread the sleeping bag over her to guard against any chill.

What could she have meant—the place where the machines come from? She must have been referring to war machines; they had certainly hadn't seen any peaceful machinery since they had arrived on this planet. But how could there possibly be a single place where all the military hardware originated? Not one source for both sides. No, the idea was impossible. If a place where machines originated really existed, it would have to be for one side or another. And even that sounded crazy. Could all the war machines on side or the other issue from a single location? This might be possible if they were coming out of underground factories. That certainly gave credence to the theory of an underground civilization.

Perhaps there were not just one, but two armed groups, both of them—staying securely below ground. While they sent their armies out to engage in battle on the surface. But what possible explanation could there be for actions of this kind? He shook his head. He was tired and could think of no solutions to any of this at the moment. Yet there *had* to be an answer, the machines and the warfare were certainly real enough.

Brion stood and looked around the crude encampment. All activity has ceased with sunset. The women were inside the cave and the Hunters were settling down to sleep in their accustomed places before the cave mouth. He looked for Ravn and found him sitting apart from the others, turning the necklace of finger bones over and over in his hands. This might be a good time to question him. Lea could be watched at the same time to make sure that she was undisturbed. Ravn would surely know something about this mysterious place of the machines.

An emotion of contentment and sleep pulsed over the settlement; anyone who threatened Lea would radiate fear, hatred, and would be instantly detected. Brion checked her again, she was still deeply asleep, then made his way through the recumbent figures to the Ravn.

"We will talk," he said. Ravn looked up, startled, clutching the necklace to him. The quick spurt of surprise was instantly replaced by cold hatred. This one would have to be watched. Always.

"It is late. The Ravn is tired. In the morning . . ."

"Now." There was no warmth in Brion's voice; he reached out and took hold the necklace for a moment, instantly aware of the man's spurt of fear. "You will do as I say. I will be obeyed at all times." He released the necklace and sat down. Ravn instantly pulled it over his head with shaking hands.

"Who am I?" Brion said. Ravn turned away, looking behind him, around, anywhere except at Brion.

"Look at me, piece of dirt. Who am I? Give me my name."

The words emerged with utmost reluctance, dripping with venom. "You are . . . Ravn Above Ravn."

"That is true. Now you will answer my questions in the same true way. You have seen machines?" A reluctant nod of the head. "Good. What kind of machines have you seen?"

"It is forbidden to talk of machines."

"It is not forbidden to talk of them to the Ravn Above Ravn. Have you seen machines that flew in the air? Good, you have. What did these machines do?"

"What machines always do. With loud noises they killed other machines, then they were killed in turn. It is always that way. That is what they do."

"Have you ever seen a machine that did not kill other machines?"

"Machines kill machines, that is what they do." The question was an impossible one to answer. It was obvious from his expression that he thought Brion was a fool for even asking it.

"All machines kill machines," Brion echoed the other's words. Then went on in the same quiet voice. "Now you will tell me—where do the machines come from?"

The words had an instant and dramatic affect on Ravn. He shuddered all over and fear replaced all his other emotions on the instant.

"You will tell me," Brion said, leaning forward and clashing his two great fists together; they impacted with a solid thud. "Tell me now!"

There was no escape. At this moment Ravn was more afraid of those fists than he was of the taboo of speaking. He pointed over his shoulder, but this did not satisfy Brion. In the end Ravn had to speak, stammering the words in a hoarse whisper.

"It is that way. Many days walking. It is there. The Place with No Name."

"You have been there?"

"Only a Ravn may visit this place. The Old Ravn showed me when I was young."

"Then you will show me since I am Ravn Above Ravn. We will go when the sun rises."

"It is forbidden . . ."

"It is forbidden to refuse me anything." He reached out to the cringing man and closed his hands about the scrawny throat. "Will you die now?" Brion forced hatred into his voice. The threat had to be real: only by deadly fear could he control the Ravn. When there was no answer he began to close his fingers with steadily increasing pressure.

Ravn gasped out the reluctant words. "We go . . . when the sun rises."

It was enough. Brion released him and returned to Lea's side without another word. She was still deeply asleep, snoring lightly, and he tried to emulate her example. But he was too aware of the emotional flow of the people around him, their spurts of sharp emotion during dreaming. And the fear and hatred hovering just below the surface at all times. In the end he realized that sleep was going to be impossible. He lay back and looked up at the stars, letting his sense of awareness reach out on all sides.

Lea woke soon after dawn. He gave her some water, then he told her what he had discovered. She nodded in agreement.

"There has to be something in it. The way the women talked, this place seemed to be very real to them, not just another historical myth."

"We will just have to go there and see for our-

selves. There has to be something out there. Ravn
was certainly reluctant enough about leading me
there. He took a lot of convincing. He was afraid of
this place of the machines as he was of me."

"Do you think he was afraid enough to run away? I
don't see him anywhere."

Lea was right; Ravn had vanished during the
night. When Brion woke the Hunters they seemed to
be as puzzled about his disappearance as he was.
They searched fitfully, some of them even scouting
down the trails leading from the encampment. But
in the end they all returned with negative reports.
Ravn had vanished without trace.

"Damn!" Brion said. "We'll never find this place
without him. I should have tied him down—he
could be miles away by now."

"I don't think so," Lea said. "In fact I have the very
strong sensation that he is a lot closer than you
imagine." She looked very smug as she stirred the
caffein extract into her cup of water, then sipped it
as it began to steam.

"Would you be so kind as to tell me just what in
hell you are talking about!"

"Temper, temper. Shouting will only raise your
blood pressure and get you nowhere." She sipped
daintily while he fumed with impatience. "Now
that's better. While you men have been stamping
around everywhere I have been watching the wom-
en. They are very afraid of something—and they
are staying inside the cave, every last one of them."

"Could he be hiding in there? Isn't it taboo for
men to go inside with the women?"

"Men, yes. The Ravn no. He even has a cache of
some kind in the rear. Want me to take a look?"

"No, that's too dangerous. My new title should get me inside as well."

The Hunters watched with mild interest as he strode towards the cave entrance—but the women retreated in panic. "I am Ravn Above Ravn!" he shouted as he bent his head to get under the overhanging ledge.

Brion blinked in the semi-darkness inside, waiting while his eyes slowly grew accustomed to it. The cave was really just a fault in the rocks, about sixty feet deep. There were cries of fear and sobbing from the women who were now all huddled together, with the children, to the back of the cave. They wailed and moved aside as he approached them. Without exception they all of them retreated to his left. Interesting. Brion went to the right, towards a stinking heap of uncured lizard skins piled high in a niche. Skins, nothing else. Or had he seen a slight movement in the darkness. He knelt and groped under the fetid mass—then shouted with delight.

Ravn wailed and slobbered as he was pulled out by the ankle, dragged clear of the skins and rolled over on the ground. Brion looked down at him, feeling a slight pity for the groveling man. But only for an instant, as he became aware of a throb of pain in his hand, where he had knocked the healing stump of his index finger against the rock floor of the cave. All trace of sympathy vanished with this and he nudged Ravn with his toe.

"Stand up, cowardly piece of filth. We start the long walk today."

Most of the morning had passed before Ravn declared himself ready to leave. There were rituals to be done, a bracelet of bones to be fetched from its hiding place in the cave, food had to be gathered. Urged on by Brion he eventually ran out of excuses and reluctantly started down the path—only to stop suddenly when he saw that Lea was following them. He waved his hands with agitation.

"No women! Women not allowed. Only Ravn can go. No hunters, no dirt women!"

"This woman comes with us only part of the way so she can carry our food for us. She will not go to the Place With No Name. She will be sent back long before that. Now—lead the way."

Dragging his feet and proceeding with the greatest reluctance, Ravn started down the hillside again. Brion and Lea followed behind him on the path through the trees, until they were well out of sight of the encampment. Brion stopped then and took the heavy bundle from Lea, slinging it across his own back. She rubbed her sore muscles. "Only dirt woman carry bundle. How come big Hunter carry big bundle? This very bad for taboo."

"Do you want it back?"

"Never! But won't dirty old Ravn protest and make trouble?"

"He couldn't hate me any more than he does now. And I can take care of any trouble he can possibly dream up. Every time I feel sorry for him my finger stump twinges and I suddenly lose all sympathy. Let me know when you get tired and we'll take a break."

"I can walk all day—as long as someone else is carrying the pack."

Their course first took them to the west, along the edge of the plain. By afternoon the foothills began to curve north along the shore of the Central Lake and they followed this natural direction of the land.

Brion called a halt before dusk, tired by a full day of walking after a sleepless night. As he had done before, he staked Ravn down so he wouldn't go wandering when they weren't watching. With the enemy well secured Brion enjoyed a deep and dreamless sleep, waking in the morning well refreshed for the trek.

They proceeded like this for three days, walking through the sparse cover of the foothills with the forest nearby. They only ventured out after dusk to fill their water bottles, if they had not crossed any streams during the day. Ravn only spoke once, shouting a warning when he heard the distant sound of engines. They lay hidden in the undergrowth watching the conrails of invisible aircraft above. The planes drew white lines across the horizon, coming from the north. If this was any indication, the march was certainly going in the right direction. Ravn was terrified of the aircraft, lying shuddering on the ground.

"We are close, too close," he insisted. "We must go back." Only with effort did Brion force him to go on. Nor did he go far. Less than an hour later he stopped and sat down under a tree.

"Now what?" Brion asked.

"We must wait until dark and then go down to the lake and pass this place by." He waved to the ridge ahead.

"We go on now," Brion ordered. "There is a lot of daylight left."

"We cannot. Up ahead is a Holy Place. We cannot go there. We must pass it by. Only at night is it safe to go along the lake."

"A Holy Place? I like the sound of that. We'll take a look . . ."

"No! It is forbidden! You cannot!"

Brion was aware of the surge of emotion that seized Ravn, a fear greater than anything he had experienced before—greater even than his fear of Brion. He screeched as he attacked, knife raised. Brion stepped inside the swinging arm, blocking the downward swing with his own arm, and caught Ravn's wrist. He seized his neck with his other hand, squeezing hard until the writhing body went limp.

"He'll be unconscious for a long time—but I'll stake him out just in case we're delayed."

"You mean while we're looking at the Holy Place?"

"No—while I'm looking at it. You'll stay with him. His fear was real. Whatever is up there is dangerous."

Lea snorted with disgust. "And just what isn't dangerous on this planet? We go together. Correct?"

Brion opened his mouth to argue—then closed it and reluctantly nodded. This was one argument that he knew he was lost even before it had begun. "Stay close to me. We have no idea what might be over the ridge."

They walked slowly upwards through the trees, then stopped at the foot of the grassy slope. It ended at the top of the ridge a few yards further on. Brion leaned close and whispered.

"Please stay here until I see what we are facing. I promise that you will join me as soon as it is safe. All right?" She nodded agreement and sank into the shelter of a large tree.

Brion crept the last few feet—an inch at a time. At the top he paused, then raised his head with infinite caution. Looked, then raised his head even higher to stare down the other side. Then he stood and waved, calling back to Lea.

"Come up here—it's all right. Just come and see what we have discovered."

THIRTEEN

The Enemy Revealed

Lea scrambled up the slope, burning with curiosity. What could it possibly be? Ravn had been deathly afraid of something up here—yet Brion was standing on the ridge, calling to her and waving. He reached down and took her hand, helping her up the last few feet. "Look," he said, pointing.

Ruins, the ancient remains of buildings of some kind. Lea shook her head.

"Is this the Holy Place? Just some decaying ruins. There is certainly nothing frightening here.

"To our eyes. This surely represents something important to the locals. They may be destroyed now, but you must realize that these are the first permanent structures of any kind that we have seen on this planet. I think that it is safe enough to take a closer look."

There was certainly nothing in the tumbled walls that could offer a threat of any kind; the ruined

buildings must have been centuries old. Some of the construction had been of steel, but this had long since rusted away leaving only red traces in the soil. However the larger buildings, great square structures, had been made of rammed earth faced with ceramic. Where the ceramic had been fractured the dirt had been washed away, but enough of it had remained intact so there was still solid structure in many places. Brion clambered up to take a closer look at one of the remaining walls, searching for any evidence that might remain of the original nature of the constructions. He kicked at the crumbling dirt, then pointed to a series of holes in the outer wall.

"Do you think it would be farfetched to suggest that these buildings might have been destroyed by explosions at one time? These could be the remains of craters—and these pockmarks in the ceramic could have been caused by fragments."

Lea nodded agreement. "More than possible, if you stop to consider what is still happening on this planet. But what could this have originally been? This place is too small to have been a city, yet these buildings are so large."

"The machinery has long since vanished—but I have a strong hunch that this could have been a mine of some kind. Those hills out there are too regular to be anything except mine tailings. These could have been the mine outbuildings and offices, with the larger structures used for storage. All destroyed by bombing. All of the people killed as well . . ."

"No! Not all of them. Isn't there a strong chance that our natives might be descendants of these people? The few survivors? Why else would they call a destroyed mine a Holy Place?"

"It's a possibility, but we have no way of telling one way or the other. They might simply have found these ruins without knowing anything about them, worshipped them for their size. Perhaps Ravn can tell us."

"I doubt it. And don't you think it's about time to go back and see if he has come around yet?"

"Yes, we've seen everything we need here. If he's still out there's no need to let him know that we have even been here. We still need his cooperation."

Ravn was awake and glaring—and refused to go on until dark. He knew where they had been, the dark flow of his hatred indicated that, but he was powerless to do anything about it. He sat, motionless, until dusk, then rose without a word and started down the hill towards the plain. They could only follow after. Half of the night had passed before they completed the large detour around the Holy Place and were back in the foothills again. They slept the remaining few hours until dawn, then pressed on.

It was early on the fourth day when they paused at one of the streams that led down to the lake, in order to refill their waterbottles. Brion stopped suddenly and looked up, his bottle still only half full. Lea saw the motion and started to speak—but he held up his hand and waved her to silence.

"Just a moment. Don't look around or draw any attention to yourself. We're not alone any more. There are some people ahead, they must be among those trees, just above that grassy slope."

"Are they friendly?"

"On this planet? Anything but. I can think of only one reason for their hiding along our trail like this. They are lying in ambush, waiting for us."

"What do we do?"

"Nothing except wait for them to show themselves and make their intentions known. If it's going to be trouble we can defend ourselves a lot better if we face them out here in the open . . ."

He pushed her suddenly to one side as something dark arced up and out from the trees. It was a long spear that thudded into the ground before them, almost at Ravn's feet. He squawked with fear.

"Well, I would say that takes care of their intentions." Lea pointed at the figures slipping out from the cover of the trees. "They look exactly like Ravn's people and we know by now what they're like. I know I shouldn't give you advice, but wouldn't you like to do something violent before they get any closer?" She tried to speak the words lightly, but could not keep the tremor out of her voice. The sight of the spear-armed men's slow advance terrified her. The violence had been ceaseless since they had landed on this planet.

"Keep behind that tree where they can't reach you," Brion called to her, as he bent to take out the container of percussion grenades. The attackers were closer, at the top of the slope now, waving their spears and shouting insults. Brion armed a grenade, waiting for them to get closer. It was stalemate for the moment—and this was when Ravn began shouting.

"I am the Ravn! I am coming to help you!"

He jumped forward into the shallow stream, still shouting, and splashed across it. Brion started forward—then drew back. It was too late to stop him now. Ravn was on the slope, waving his arms and shouting.

"There are two of them, behind me, hiding, kill

them, I will help. They have touched metal, they have machines! I have seen them. They must be destroyed!''

His words brought the spearmen forward, their voices rising to match his. They could see his necklace and bracelet, they knew that he was a Ravn, they would obey . . .

Flame and smoke erupted suddenly from the hillside, sending metal fragments sleeting through the boughs and into the trees. Ravn was lifted from his feet, broken, hurled aside. The sound of the explosion crashed out, and in the silence that followed, the wail of the retreating hunters keened loudly. Even as Brion hurled himself to the ground, dragging Lea with him, a second explosion hurled bro-

ken boughs and fragments of tree trunk from the
forest above. This time Brion was aware of an echo-
ing explosion from the plain behind them, and
turned to see an armored tank drawn up beside the
stream. It's long gun, pointing in their direction,
vanished suddenly behind a cloud of flame-pierced
smoke. The third shell struck even further up among
the trees where the men had disappeared.

As suddenly as it had begun, the firing stopped.
The scarred slope was empty except for the huddled
corpse. The Hunters were gone. Without a visible
target the operator nosed the gun back and forth—
then the tank spun away as the turret was traversed.
Dust spurted from the treads as the tank got under
way.

"Don't move until it's out of sight," Brion said. "We don't know what kind of detectors it has aboard. I don't know who is manning that thing, but they certainly don't seem to like the natives."

"Could they possibly be the same people, their descendents I mean, of the ones who destroyed that mine we found?"

"There is every possibility . . . wait, look!"

High above them the sun glinted on silver wings, diving downwards. One instant the two aircraft were tiny specks, a moment later they grew to dart-shaped forms that dived faster than the speed of sound. Down they came, one behind the other, aiming for the solitary tank. The tank operator must have detected them as well because it spun about on its treads, but it was too late. Dark specks separated from the planes as they soared upwards again in tight arcs. Explosions hid the tank from sight as the squealing roar of the jets tore at their ears. There was silence as the smoke and dust drifted slowly away, revealing the shattered and smoking ruin of the tank.

Brion put his arm about Lea, helping her to her feet, feeling the trembling of her slim body.

"It's all right, it's over now. We're not hurt."

"It's impossible. I can't stand this place any more. Nothing but violence and death and killing . . ." Her voice broke; he kept his arm about her.

"We knew that before we came. We made the choice. All we can do now is finish the job. Do what must be done . . ."

She pushed his arm away from her. "You're a sanctimonious swine! Unfeeling and uncaring— with as much human feeling as a piece of wood. Don't touch me . . ."

He obeyed her, knowing that was all he could do for the moment. He was trained for stress, his planet was a harsh and brutal one, while Lea came from an overcrowded and overcivilized world. She had been forced to come too far, too quickly. Now she needed some time to recover.

They were secure in the trees, so the best thing they could do for the moment was remain in hiding until they were absolutely sure the sudden, deadly conflict was definitely over. He opened the bag and found the vodka. He poured out a cupful, and brought it over to her. She took it without a word, her face strained and white, and sipped from it. Brion went past her to the edge of the grove and looked out across the plain. It was empty and silent save for the smoking ruin of the tank.

"What do we do next?" she asked, coming up behind him.

"Send for the ship. Get you to safety."

"Is it wise to land the lifeship here?"

"No. But we have little choice. I cannot submit you to these conditions any longer."

Lea dug a small plastic comb from her pocket and pulled it through the worse tangles of her hair. "It's a little late to turn back. I don't like it—but I do remember that I volunteered. Despite your protests. I made this bed, so I had better learn to lie in it."

"You don't have to."

"Yes I do. I'm the wrong sex for all the macho and big strong man sort of thing, but I still have my pride. When you stop to think about it, after that last planet we were on this one really is a picnic spot. Isn't it time to go on?"

Brion realized that there was nothing he could say. Silence was really the only answer now. She knew what she was doing, knew how she felt and what the risks were. He may have had all of the brawn—but he realized suddenly that her determination was the same as his. Or stronger. She would see that the job was finished.

"I want to take a closer look at that tank," he said, later, after the flames had died and the dust long settled. She nodded.

"Of course. There'll be records, fragments of clothing, identification, something. It's about time we did something beside mix with the natives. When should we go?"

He shook his head. "There's no 'we' this time. One person will go out there, the other will have to stay here with the radio to make a report. I think it best if you stay with the radio. I'll take the holocamera and work fast, just in and out. I'll set it to automatic and it will shoot a hundred frame roll in less than fifteen seconds."

"Don't think that I'm going to argue with you. I know that you can do the reconaissance faster and better than I ever could. Should you wait—or go now?"

Brion looked up at the sky and nodded. "Now I think. The local tribe are frightened off for the time being, so there will be no trouble from them. And I'll need light, so I can't wait until after dark. There are no other tanks in sight—and the aircraft are an unknown factor. I want to get out there and back as quickly as I can. It shouldn't take long."

He was gone on the instant, running at top speed, making directly for the wreck. It was time to make a preliminary report. Lea took the radio out and described the events of the day as clearly as she could, then switched off. She saw that Brion had fallen flat beside the tank and was lying there motionless. Then he moved and vanished out of sight behind the machine.

It was hard to wait. Although she knew that the local tribe were long gone she listened to every rustle and crack in the forest behind, waiting for footsteps. The sky and the plain remained empty. Slow seconds crept by.

And there he was—running back! She had never seen a more beautiful sight in her entire life than that great hurtling shape. Pounding through the thick grass and on into the security of the trees, coming through them back to her side. He was breathing heavily, his skin dripping with sweat.

"Didn't suspect this . . ." he said, leaning against the tree next to her.

"Suspect what? Who was driving that tank?"

"No one. That is the awful part. It's empty . . . empty of human beings at least. The tank was completely robot controlled. Operated by robots guidance trained to seek out and kill people. That's who is fighting this war, fighting on one side at least.

"A mechanized army of killer robots."

FOURTEEN

Machines That Murder

A small red light that had been blinking on the rear of the holocamera changed to green, indicating that the development cycle was complete. Brion took out the roll of film and slipped it into the holder of the projector. When he switched it on a jagged wall of metal instantly appeared in the opening between the trees. It floated there, against all reason, a holographic projection indistinguishable from the real thing.

"This is a shot of the outside of the tank," Brion said, pressing the actuator button. "And here is what I saw when I first looked in."

The projected image vanished and another took its place; the interior of the ruined tank. Flying shrapnel had cut up the apparatus, but the units were still identifiable. Brion pointed to the jumble of cables and circuit boxes.

"This is the view facing forward. You'll notice

that there are no seats or controls for human operators. Just these inputs and microprocessors. The whole interior is so cramped that it must have been designed solely for robot control. See that metal tube? That's the ammunition feed for the recoilless canon. It goes right across the interior, right through the space where a human gunner or driver would sit. But there is more than enough space to site the control units for robot operation."

"I don't understand. How can this be possible?" Lea said. "I thought that robots were incapable of injuring people? There are the robotic laws . . ."

"Perhaps on Earth, but they were never applied out at the fringes of the old Earth Empire. You are forgetting that robots are machines, nothing more. They are not human so we shouldn't be anthropomorphic about them. They do whatever they are programmed to do—and do it without emotional reactions of any kind. They have been used in combat ever since technological warfare began. To aim bombs, warn of approaching aircraft, guide missiles, fire guns, a hundred different tasks. And what they do they do faster and better than a human being. Add to this the fact that they are far more rugged in every way, and you will understand why the military like them. You'll find that the history of the wars during the Breakdown is filled with references to battles that were almost fully automated. They were tremendously wasteful—but at least they were not deadly to human beings. Only when one side was defeated, or ran out of material, did the human populations suffer. But once the mechanized defenses were breached the defeated side usually surrendered quite quickly."

"Then the war robots didn't mind killing people . . ."

"They couldn't *mind* because they are incapable of emotions. They simply obey instructions. That robot tank had been programmed to look for people—then destroy them. We saw how good it was at its task."

"But people must have programmed it. So they are morally responsible for the killing, aren't they?"

"Absolutely. They are the real criminals who should be brought to justice."

Lea watched with growing distaste as the images of the shattered war machine flickered and changed. "At least this killer-robot has been destroyed. Perhaps that is what is going on out there, what this war is all about. The pilots of those aircraft were trying to stop these robots."

"They were—but how do you know that there were pilots in the jets? They could have been robots too."

"That's crazy. A war of robots fighting robots on a virtually uninhabited planet, and incidentally shooting up the surviving people at the same time. It doesn't make sense."

"It may not make sense to us—but it's happening out there, you can't deny that. Those war machines must come from some place on this planet."

"Underground factories?"

"Perhaps. We've chewed that one over before. We are just going to have to keep looking for the Place With No Name."

"I'm not going to lie and say that I miss him, but isn't that going to be difficult with Ravn dead?"

"Difficult, but not impossible. We'll just keep

pushing north, staying under cover of the forest as much as we can. We have just had evidence of what could happen to us if we are seen."

"Wouldn't it be better to travel at night?"

"No. We're safer by daylight. Whatever kind of detection equipment the machines use, radio location, infrared, heat monitors, anything, the devices will work just as well in the dark. While we have to depend upon vision alone. My empathetic sense will enable us to avoid the tribesmen, but is no good in detecting the machines. So we'll move by day to enable us to keep our eyes open for the war machines, to see them before they spot us."

Although the tension and the danger were still there, the journey was easier without the venomous presence of Ravn. He had died while trying to betray them; he would not be missed. Their course was almost due north now, with the great inland sea off to their right at all times. They stayed among the trees and paralleled the open plain. As the days passed they saw fewer and fewer animals grazing there, perhaps because the military presence was now much greater. Aircraft passed over at least once a day, swinging in wide circles as though searching for something. One night there was a battle of some kind over the horizon; distant explosions shook the ground and they could see the flare of explosions against the clouds.

It was a day later that the war column passed. They saw the clouds of dust clearly building up to the north, quickly billowing even higher. At first it resembled a sandstorm—but this was grassy plain, not desert, and there was nothing natural about this steady advance.

"Up among the trees, quickly," Brion said, leading the way with ground-eating strides. "There's a ridge up there. We want to be behind it—with solid stone between us and their detection equipment if that's what I think it is."

He threw the bundle down among the rocks, then helped Lea the rest of the way up the hill. There were great jumbled boulders here, and they wormed their way into the space under one of the largest, completely concealing themselves. Brion pushed the bundle with the metal apparatus even further down to make it as indetectable as possible. Then he piled up the flatter rocks into a rough shelter, leaving thin openings through which they could peer out.

"I can hear them now," Lea said." All that rumbling and rattling. Here they come!"

Dark masses were visible now, running in front of the dust clouds, growing larger and ever larger as they came on. Massive forms, heavily armored and armed weapons of war. Smaller and more agile machines were soon visible, darting back and forth, flanking them on all sides. These covering forces were everywhere, spreading out and nosing along the lake shore and even up to the hillside. Lea cringed down in their hiding place as a flight of jets roared low over their heads; the trailing explosion of their supersonic flight crashed down upon the stone shelter. As the armada advanced the plain became black with fighting machines. As far as they could see it was thickly covered with the engines of war. Their ears ached with the metallic roar.

It was late afternoon before the main body of the armored column had passed, but squads of the smaller and faster tanks still coursed about in their wake.

"That was quite a display," Lea said.

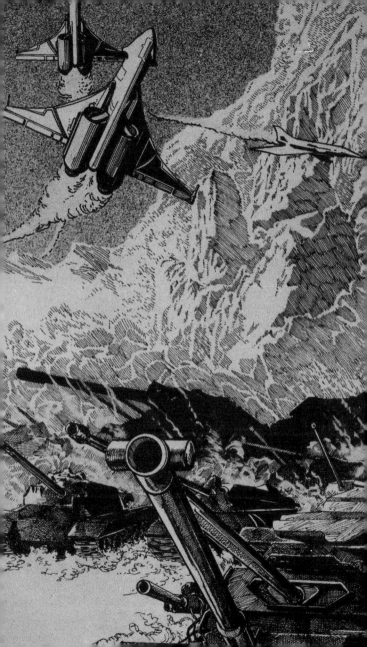

"An inhuman one. Out there was nothing but machines. Programmed machines. If there had been human operators driving those things I would have sensed their massed emotions, even at this distance. But there was absolutely nothing."

"Couldn't there have been a few people there, somewhere among the machines? In control?"

"Very possible, I wouldn't have detected their presence. But even if there were a handful of human beings guiding that column I would say that ninety-five, ninety-eight percent of the machines had to be robot operated."

"It's frightening . . ."

"Everything about this operation is frightening. And deadly. We're going to stay here until morning. I want those machines to get as far away from us as possible before we move on. One good thing about this, at least we know which way we have to go now."

"What do you mean?"

Brion pointed out the great scars that had been ground into the plain by the passing of the mechanized army. "They left a trail that we could follow blindfolded. We are going to backtrack them—find out where they came from."

"We can't! There may be still more of them coming from the same direction."

"We will stay well out of their way. Those tracks can be seen for miles so we won't have to keep too close to them. We'll move with caution as we have been doing. But we are going to follow their tracks for as long as we have to. We are not going to stop until we find where those machines came from."

For the first few days there were no problems. But

after that the tracking became more and more difficult to do. Once the Central Lake had disappeared
from view behind them, the nature of the countryside began to gradually change. There was no
longer the continuous sequence of mountains,
wooded foothills and grassy plain. The terrain became more broken and mountainous with the hills
cut through by valleys and gorges. Brion stopped on
the steep hillside, looking out at the sharp-cut tracks
dug into the plain. They were still clearly visible on
the plain below, but disappearing from sight where
they vanished into the mouth of a steep-sided gorge.

"What do we do now?" Lea said.

"Have something to eat while we do some serious
thinking. I suppose it might just be possible to take
to the hills and follow along above the track."

She looked up at the towering cliff and sniffed. "A
lot easier said then done." She broke out a ration
pack then held out the almost empty container.
"And if you will notice—we are also running out of
food. Whatever happens, we are going to have to
turn back fairly soon, or send for the lifeship so we
can resupply."

"I don't like either choice. We've come this far and
we are still on their trail. We must go on. We can't
resupply because we don't dare risk landing the ship
in an area with so many fighting machines about.
Which leaves a single option open . . ."

"Don't say it. Just open the mouth to put in food.
And then we will follow my plan. We will go back to
the plain, bring the ship down and get back into
orbit where we know we will be safe. We have plenty
to report. After that we sit tight and wait for them to
send the troops in . . ."

Brion shook his head in a firm no. "We *are* the troops. And we can't leave until we find out just what is happening here. So that leaves us with a single remaining course open. Into the canyon . . ."

"You're out of your mind. That is certain suicide."

"I don't think so. I see it more as a fifty-fifty chance. A fast move, in and out before any more machines come this way."

"And I can just see what is coming next. This is going to be a one-man crash operation, isn't it? With you on foot wearing your running shoes and waving your big transparent dagger. While I sit it out here with all the metallic equipment, waiting patiently for your return."

"That's the sort of scenario I had in mind. Can you find anything wrong with it?"

"Just one thing. Wouldn't it be a lot easier to simply blow your own brains out and save yourself all that trouble?"

He took her small hand in his large one, clearly sensing the worry and fear behind her harsh words. "I know what you are thinking and feeling, and I can't blame you for it. But at this moment in time we don't really have a choice. It's either turn back and start the whole operation over again. Or finish it now. I've think we've come too far, been involved in too much violence and bloodshed to drop it all now. I can take care of myself. And I need to see this thing right through to the end."

There was no point in arguing, Lea understood that and was possessed by a sensation of dark resignation. They packed the bag in silence and moved deeper into the hills, away from the canyon, until they found a suitable campsight. It had a sheltered overhang of stone and was just above a rushing mountain stream.

"You'll be safe here," Brion said, handing her the rapid-fire pistol. "Keep this near you at all times. If you see anything at all you must shoot first and investigate later. There is nothing friendly out here, animals, machines—or men. I'll give you plenty of warning when I get back, so don't worry about shooting me."

The night was cool, for the first time, here in the hills. They shared the sleeping bag for warmth. Brion fell asleep instantly, years of training had taught him to do that, but sleep did not come that easily for her. She lay awake far into the night, staring up through the canopy of the trees at the alien, star-filled heavens, so different from the sky of Earth. She was such a long way from home.

Lea woke to a touch on her shoulder to find that it was light. Brion stood over her, securing his knife into place.

"In the last report I am sure that we recorded everything of importance that we have learned so far, so you will be able to keep radio silence. And you must stay under cover at all times. This is day one—and I'll be back at the very latest by the evening of day four. I promise to return no matter what I find in there. If I'm not back at the promised time you must not wait for me. And I'm sure that you realize what folly it would be to follow me. Whether I'm here or not you must start back on day five. Bring down the lifeship as soon as you reach the plain—then get off of this planet. Fast. There are other agents who can crack this nut if we fail. But don't concern yourself with these contingency plans. I'll see you here in four days."

He turned on his heel and was gone. Quickly, before she could say a thing. It was obvious that he preferred it that way. She watched his great form lope easily away down the bank of the stream, growing smaller and smaller until he dropped over a ledge and was gone from sight.

FIFTEEN

Canyon Quest

There was no logical reason to hesitate at the mouth of the canyon—but logic had nothing to do with this. Brion jumped down the last few feet from the terraced hillside—then stopped. Unmoving. Listening to the silence. On each side of him the high walls of stone rose up to form a natural corridor that sliced deep into the hillside. He could see about a quarter of a mile ahead before a turn in the canyon concealed the rest of it from sight. The ground before him had once been covered with grass and shrubs, but these had long since been pulverized and ground into rutted soil. Only a few bits of greenery remained close to the rocky walls. The rest had been churned up and destroyed under the tracks of the advancing army. Machine after machine had chewed into the stony ground until it was a tumbled sea of overlapping tracks. When Brion looked down he saw that he was standing in one of the deep marks, an indentation that was more than a yard square. And this was just one part of the track of the gigantic machine—that in itself was only one of a legion. And army of machines had passed this way, and for all he knew more of them could be coming towards him at this very moment. And he was going to tackle this machine army—singlehanded?

"Yes!" he shouted aloud, smiling wryly at the same time. The odds weren't too good—but they were the only odds that he was going to get. And with every passing instant that he stood there they were getting longer, since the chance that he might meet the enemy in this narrow canyon grew more and more possible. He started forward at a faster ground-eating trot.

The rocky walls of the canyon slipped steadily by; the churned up ground was rutted and uneven underfoot. After almost an hour of steady running he found that he was beginning to breathe heavily, so he slowed to a fast walk. He continued this way until he had got his wind back, then increased his pace again. The miles passed, one after another, the canyon was featureless and unchanging. It was mid-afternoon before the walls of rock receded as he emerged into a rocky bowl in the mountains.

This was a good opportunity to take a break. For the first time he left the well-marked track and clambered up the grassy patches between the tumbled boulders. From here the churned highway was clearly visible, crossing the bowl and disappearing into another valley mouth on the far side. After drinking a few mouthfuls of water he lay back and closed his eyes. An hour's sleep, then he would go on. It was getting more chill at this altitude so it might be more comfortable to do his sleeping during the day, then keep going through the night. He knew that his personal metabolism could easily adapt to this. At home, on Havrk, food had to be gathered during the brief summer to prepare for the very long winter. He had gone four and five days without sleep and knew that he could do it again any time. The grass was soft, while the niche in the rocks was protected from the wind and warmed by the sun. He settled down and was asleep within a few moments.

At the appointed time his eyes opened and he looked up at the cloudless sky. The sun had dropped behind the hills and it was growing cool in the shade. The track below him was still empty. He seated his knife comfortably on his hip, took the smallest sip of water—and went on.

This canyon was wider now, but the bends were sharper and prevented him from seeing very far ahead. He slowed down for each corner, going around it cautiously—until he realized that he was wasting too much time this way. What would happen would happen, he could not avoid it. He had to press on and be more fatalistic about the future.

The floor of the valley had changed to hard rock, scratched and gouged by the steel treads, but still far smoother than the ploughed-up soil below. As he adjusted to the rhythm of the constant motion he found his progress steady, his breathing strong and regular. Almost relaxed. He pounded steadily around a sharp bend and saw the armored vehicle just a few yards ahead.

It had a machine's reflexes. The four-gunned turret had been pointed towards the sky. Now, with frightening speed it slewed about and pointed di-

rectly at him. Even as he dived back for the shelter of
the rock he saw those four dark mouths gaping. The
shells would strike him in the back, they could not
miss . . .

He landed and rolled and pushed himself against
the unyielding stone, surprised that he was still
alive. Nothing had happened. The guns had not
fired.

Brion lay there, his breath rasping hard, waiting
for the clank of treads as the machine started forward. He knew that he could not outrun it. Could he
climb out of this trap? No, the valley walls were
smooth and precipitous. There was no escape.

The sound of its motor was loud and harsh. Metal

screeched and echoed and the motor raced unevenly.

Then the sound died away leaving an aching silence. The thing wasn't coming for him—but it was still blocking his way. Why had it stopped?

Brion took a deep and shuddering breath, then climbed slowly to his feet. He had been spared—but for how long. What was he to do? It would be dark soon. Perhaps he could get by the tank in the dark. No, the darkness would mean nothing to the machine; it senses would be just as alert then. Go back? He could—but it would mean the end. Giving up. He had come too far to do that now. And why hadn't the thing fired at him? Curiosity got the better of caution.

Ever so slowly, a fraction of an inch at a time, he crawled forward over the rocks. Raising his head over the top . . .

Falling back as he found himself looking directly into the muzzles of the guns.

Yet still they hadn't fired. The thing knew that he was here—so why was it hesitating? Some sort of cat and mouse game? No, it wouldn't be programmed for anything except destruction. Then what should he do?

He picked up a fair-sized rock, drew it far back—then hurled it up and out with a straight-armed grenade throw. It hit the ground with a resounding crash and he raised his head again as it did.

Gears ground as the gun turret pointed at the rock, then whined again as it spun back to sight on him. This time he did not move. The machine already had had two chances to kill him—and nothing had happened. This was the third. If it fired now at least he would never know it.

One second, two, then three slipped by. The guns were still silent. Emboldened he stepped out from behind cover and started forward. The guns turned slowly, never leaving him as he advanced.

Brion stopped as the engine rumbled again and the tank vibrated, clanking forward a few inches, then stopped. That was when he noticed for the first time that it had shed one of its tracks and could not move.

If he could get past the thing it would not be able to follow him! He ran, straight up the valley, painfully aware of the guns tracking him every inch of the way. Only when he was even with the machine, passing it, did the guns suddenly stop moving. Then the turret ground slowly around and the guns drifted back to the vertical. Brion stopped as well and looked at the thing.

It was ignoring him now. He must have passed out of range of the forward-facing sensors and his presence had been wiped from its memory banks. Should he take the time to go closer, to examine it?

There was no way he could justify the action other than curiosity. The release from tension, and the fear of certain death that had so recently overwhelmed him, had made him almost lightheaded and fearless for the moment. He had to get closer to the thing, to look at it. It might reveal something, or nothing, it didn't really matter.

He approached it, step by cautious step, but the machine paid him no need. He was close enough now to see the weld marks on its metal hide, to put one foot on the shining metal of a bogey wheel and clamber up its side. There was a hatch on top, just behind the gun turret, with a single locking handle.

He hesitated a second—then reached out and pulled down on it, hard.

Soundlessly and effortlessly the hatch swung open.

Nothing else happened. Brion heard his heart hammering loudly as he leaned forward and looked in. The tank was empty of life. Instruments glowed in the half-darkness; somewhere a servo motor hummed and then was still. Festoons of ammunition rose up to the guns beside him. They were armed and ready to fire. Then why hadn't they fired at him?

Enough! He was suddenly angry at himself for this stupidity. What was he doing here—risking his life without reason? He had passed the war machine safely. All he should have done was continue on his way, to get as far away from the thing as he could. He kicked out at the steel side with disgust at himself, then jumped down and ran steadily up the valley, never looking back.

This was one more puzzle to add to the rest of the puzzles that seemed to make up this deadly world. And none of these puzzles would be solved unless he discovered the origin of the army that had passed them. He ran on.

He was still moving when darkness fell, but he kept running steadily, the ground clearly visible by starlight. It was a merciless grind even for him, and long before the night was over he stopped for a rest. Then another one. Fatigue was slowing him when he reached a narrow side canyon. He got down on his knees to examine the ground carefully, but were no track marks leading from it. The canyon should provide a safe place to rest. He walked into it, until he was well out of sight of the valley below, then found shelter between two large boulders and was instantly asleep.

Sometime later a disturbance drew him from his deep sleep. The stars shown brightly above, stretching from horizon to horizon. He could hear nothing from the valley—but far distant the sound of jet engines was clearly audible, dying slowly away. It had nothing to do with him. He closed his eyes and when he opened them again the sky was gray with dawn.

He was tired and chill, his muscles sore. The water was icy in his mouth and he resisted the urge to drink more than a few carefully rationed sips. And he was hungry. He had expected these reactions so he determinedly forced his attention away from such weaknesses. The job still had to be done. Once he started moving he would warm up; thirst and hunger could be lived with. He must press on.

When the valley began to widen out he stayed close to the eastern wall, moving through the shadow. This might provide him some protection if he should meet more of the machines. The valley began to grow level, becoming wider at the same time, the surface growing harder as he went. Changing from packed soil and rock to something harder and smoother. He bent to examine it.

It was solidified molten rock. Not rounded and lumpy as it would have been had it been formed by natural volcanic action, but smooth and level. It had been melted by fusion guns, then leveled into place.

The surface of the valley was artificial.

The sun was higher in the sky now and was clear of the shadowing ridge. It lit up the entire valley floor, revealing its artificially smooth and flattened surface. Brion walked over it cautiously, examining the rocky walls on both sides at the same time. They were completly smooth and solid, without openings of any kind, even at the valley end.

Nothing. The rock walls were ancient, natural. This was a dead end. A box valley that began here and extended down to the plains. A rock-walled slice through the mountains with only the single exit.

Yet he knew that a mighty mechanical army had poured out of this valley. He had seen it himself and backtracked it to this spot. How could there be nothing here? It was impossible.

He walked slowly over to the rock wall and reached up and touched it, then beat against it with the hilt of his knife in frustrated rage. It was solid. This just could not be possible. Yet it was.

When he turned about to look back down the valley he saw the dark column for the first time. It was less than four feet high and stood about ten yards out from the rear wall. He walked slowly towards it, around it—then reached out and touched it. It was metal, an alloy of some kind, slightly worn by time, with its surface lightly tarnished. It had no markings, could have no function that he was aware of. He could scratch it with the tip of his knife; it left a bright line when he pulled it across the rounded top. As he put the knife carefully back into the sheath he felt his anger and frustration rising.

"What is it?" he bellowed at the top of his lungs. "What is the meaning of all this?"

His words echoed and bounced from the rocky walls and died away until the valley was still again.

SIXTEEN

Secret of the Black Column

In a rage of impotent fury, Brion kicked out at the dark column. This produced only a dull thud and a sharp pain in his foot.

"Very impressive, Brion," he said aloud. "The considered reactions of an intelligent man. Feeling better? Now that you have gotten rid of your temper—and have a sore foot to prove it—isn't it time to give a little thought to this problem? It is. Now what do you know? To begin with, point number one," he raised a finger, "the mechanized army came out of this valley. There can be no doubt about that. The tracks I followed all led to this spot. There were no turnings or alternative routes. Which leads to conclusion number two—the machines *must* have come from here, from this end of the valley, the area right here where I'm standing. The cliffs and the ground appear to be solid—but maybe they are not. To be examined. But what about a closer look at this column first? It is artificial, made of metal—and the chances are a hundred to one that it has something to do with this problem. So, number three, examination of column is on top of the list."

Something was nagging at his memory. What was it? When he had kicked the column, aside from hurting his toe, there had been something about it? But what? *Yes*, of course, it had sounded as though it might have been hollow, giving out more of a ring than a thud when his boot had hit it.

Brion took out his knife and reversed it. Holding it by the blade, he rapped the pommel on the top of the column, where he had scratched the metal. This produced a solid thud. But when he tapped it further down it rang loudly. It *was* hollow!

Which instantly prompted a second question: was it a hollow shell with something inside of it? A decided possibility. He must look for some way to open it, to get inside.

Brion ran his fingers slowly down the side of the column; it was smooth and unmarked. He got down on his knees to examine the lower half, then lay flat on the ground to look at the bottom. Was that a hairline crack around the base? He pushed hard with the tip of his blade—and it went under the metal! The crack was there, running all the way around the base. Although the column was apparently sunk into the solid stone—in reality it appeared to have a casing that rested on the surface. As he straightened up something caught his eye, a silvery glint of light, about a foot above the ground.

It was a scratch in the metal.

A closer examination revealed the fact that the scratch had been caused by something that had been fitted into a slot about an inch long—a slot with a scribed circle around it.

"A screw head! It looks just like a large screw head. And screws are meant to be turned."

The only tool he had with him was the knife: it would have to do. He pressed the sharp tip into the groove, then pushed down on the handle. Nothing happened. Harder. He could feel his muscles knot with the strain, could see the knife blade bend. It might snap. That didn't matter. Harder still . . .

With a metallic creak the circular piece of metal rotated a fraction of an inch. When he ran his finger over the surface he could feel that it projected slightly; a metal plug, no longer flush with the surface. Now that it had been started, it turned more easily. Around and around, until the head was clear and he could see the shining screw threads below it. More and more—so loose now that he could turn it with his fingers. He twisted it out and dropped it to the ground, then bent over and peered into the opening. Blackness, nothing visible. But the bolt *must* have had some function. Did it hold something in place? What?

He raised the knife to probe the opening with the tip, then thought better of it. It would be far wiser to use his brains than just to probe at random. What had the function of the plug been? Was it designed to cover an opening, with a control of some kind inside it? Possible, but highly improbable. Perhaps it held the outer tube of the column into place? That seemed like a more reasonable possibility.

He bent over and jammed the knife blade against the bottom of the metal tube and managed to force it under a bit, then pulled up. It moved!

By levering back and forth, Brion managed to

push the knife blade in as far as it would go, about a half an inch. The tube must now be free to move up and down. He left the knife in position and leaned over to embrace the foot-thick tube, bending his knees and wrapping his arms about it. Holding it to him as tightly as he could—he slowly straightened his legs.

Something moved. The metal tube had lifted slightly from the ground. He looked down and saw that it was a good half inch off the stone surface now, still supported by something on the inside. Moving precisely and carefully, so the thing would not drop back, he shifted his grip down and lifted again.

It rose slowly, an inch at a time, until he had raised it a good foot above the ground. He caught a glimpse of a shiny metal surface inside.

Bit by bit he lifted it higher, until he could get his fingertips under the bottom edge. Once this grip was secure he bent his legs until he was squatting on his thighs, took a deep breath and straightened up, lifting smoothly. The metal tube rose up and up—then dropped suddenly sideways as it came free.

Brion jumped back as it clanged down on the stone surface. Breathing deeply as he looked at what had been revealed.

Fitted inside a shiny metal frame was a compact electronic apparatus of some kind. There were familiar looking circuit boards with memory nodules, amplifiers and transformers, and all of it connected together by a network of wires. A thick cable emerged from a junction box, and he traced it with his eye down to the solid bulk of an atomic battery that was fitted into place at the base. It was a heavy duty battery which meant that if the drain

wasn't too great this machine might be able to function for years without attention. But what *was* its function? Almost all of the components were familiar, resembling closely some he had worked with himself. As he looked at it, Brion became aware of a slight humming emanating from the device. Was it functioning? He walked around it and, yes, there were LED displays on the far side, flickering with swift-changing numbers. So it was working, fine. But what *was* it—and what possible connection did it have to do with the war machines?

Brion bent and picked up his knife, then stepped back to look at the thing again. It was an absolute mystery. He raised the blade and aimed it, filled with the sudden impulse to jam it deep into the works. He resisted. That would accomplish nothing, other than his possible electrocution. Could there possibly be any nameplates or identification marks of any kind on the thing? As he bent over for a closer look loud explosions boomed out close behind him.

Reflex sent him hurtling to one side, rolling as he fell, turning and raising the knife before him.

Three men stood there, facing him, men who could not possibly have been there an instant before.

Three men dressed completely in black, with heavy boots and thick pressure suits. Their features were concealed by helmets with reflecting faceplates. All of them carried metal cases of some kind, and they did not appear to be armed. They must have been equally surprised to see him, for they recoiled back from the threat of his knife. Brion straightened slowly and slid the knife back into its sheath and took a step towards the nearest man. The man stepped back and pressed a control at his waist.

There was a sharp bang—and he vanished just as suddenly as he had appeared.

"What's happening here? Who are you?" Brion called out, walking forward. The two remaining men fell back before him just as explosions sounded for a third time. They were cracked out in rapid sucession as, one after another, and at least a dozen more men appeared dressed in the same outfits.

But these men were armed. Their heavy rifles were raised and pointed in his direction. Brion stood still, making no movements to alarm them. The man in front, with identifying stripes of some kind on his arms, lowered his weapon and touched his helmet. His faceplate opened.

"Who are you?" he said. "What are you doing here?"

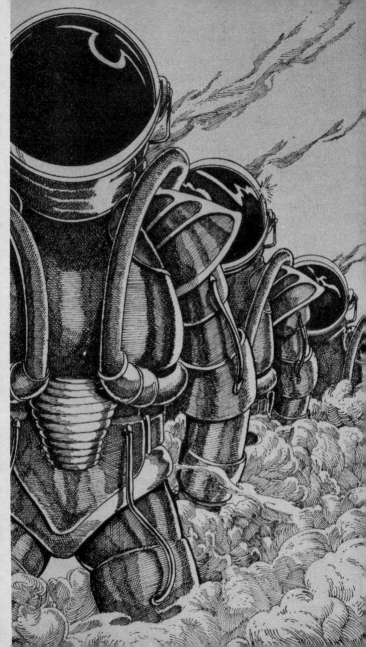

SEVENTEEN

The Killers

The other armed men were opening their face-plates now.

"Does he understand you, sergeant?" one of them called out.

"That's a wicked looked knife he's wearing."

"Tell him to drop it."

Brion understood well enough; they were speaking Universal Esperanto, the interstellar language that everyone used in addition to their native tongue. He raised his hand slowly and placed it carefully on his knife. "I'm going to put this on the ground. Just keep your fingers easy on those triggers."

The Sergeant watched closely, gun pointed, as Brion dropped the knife. When it was on the ground he lowered his gun and stepped forward. He was a grim looking man with slitted eyes, his skin pale above the black smudge of his unshaven jaw.

"You're not a Gyongyos tech," the Sergeant said. "Not in that outfit. What are you doing here?"

"I was about to ask you the same question, Sergeant," Brion said. "Explain yourself. I have more questions than you do . . ."

"Not for me you don't. I don't like this at all." He called back over his shoulder. "Corporal. Jump back and get a pressure suit, a big one. Tell the captain what we've found, tell him to let the War Department know at once."

The crackling explosion sounded again. Brion realized it had something to do with their appearence and disappearence, as though they moved so fast they displaced the air, or left a vacuum like a lightning bolt. Military ranks, reporting to the War Department—they must surely have some connection with the mechanized army that had originated here. Perhaps the machines had materialized just the way they did!

"You're responsible for the tanks and all the armored vehicles, aren't you?"

The Sergeant raised his gun. "I'm responsible for nothing—except following orders. Now just shut up until you are off my hands. If you want to talk, talk to Intelligence. That'll make everybody happy."

Despite the threat of the guns, Brion was overwhelmed by a feeling of success. There *had* to be a relationship between these people and this embattled planet. The solution was close at hand; he must control his impatience. He watched intently while the technicians, the first group to arrive, worked on the instrument that had been concealed in the heart of the metal column. They hooked leads and meters to it, and appeared to be testing various units and functions. It must have operated correctly because they quickly disconnected their machines, then lifted the metal cover back into place. When it was seating firmly they allligned the opening, then replaced the sealing bolt he had removed. Brion itched to question them, but forced himself to silence. The opportunity would come soon enough. He turned as the familiar crackling bang sounded again. The Corporal had returned with a bundled suit under his arm.

"Lieutenant says to bring him in, got a reception waiting. Here's the suit."

The promised reception sounded ominous, but Brion had little choice under the muzzles of the pointing guns. He put the suit on as directed, sealing himself into it. The sergeant slammed the faceplate shut and reached for one of the controls on at Brion's waist. There was a twisting sensation, impossible to describe, and everything changed on the instant. The valley and the soldiers were gone—and he was standing on a metal platform. Bright lights glared down and uniformed soldiers were running towards him. They unsealed the suit and stripped it from him under the supervision of a young officer.

"Come with me," he ordered Brion. There was no point in protesting at this point; he went quietly. He had a quick glimpse of massive machinery, with heavy wires looping from insulators as thick as his body, before being hustled through a metal door and down the corridor beyond. It was painted a neutral gray, with a number of doors along its length. They stopped before one labeled CORPS 3, opened it and waved Brion inside. He went in and heard it shut behind him.

"Sit in that chair, if you please," a man said in a quiet voice. He was in a chair of his own, no more than two yards away from Brion. A thin man with pale, drawn skin, his cheekbones clearly outlined below his deepset eyes, dressed in neutral gray. He smiled at Brion, but it was only a gesture, a movement of the face with no warmth or sincerity behind it. Brion could hear him clearly although they were separated by a transparent wall that divided the small room in half. Brion lowered himself into the chair, the only object of any kind on his side of the barrier.

"I have some questions for you," Brion said.

"I am sure that you do. And I for you. Shall we do our best to satisfy one another? I am Colonel Hegedus, Opole People's Army. And you?"

"My name is Brion Brandd. Do I take it then that Corps 3 is military intelligence?"

"It is. How very observing of you. We have no intention of causing you any harm, Brion. We are just very interested in what you planned to do with the Delta Beacon that you had dismantled."

"Is that what it is called? I was investigating it because I thought it might have something to do with the war on Selm-II."

"Are you telling me that you are a spy of some kind?"

"Are you telling me that there is something on this planet for me to spy upon?"

"Please, Brion, don't let us play games. The area where you were found is of great strategic importance as you well know. If you are with Gyongyos intelligence you had better tell me—you know how easily we can find out the truth from you."

"I'm afraid that I haven't the slightest idea what you are talking about. The truth is that I am completely mystified by what has happened. I arrived on this planet in the midst of a devastating war . . ."

"Excuse me, but there is no war on this planet, you know that . . ." For the first time real emotion shown on Hegedus's face; sudden shock. "No, you don't know that, do you. You still think you are on Selm-II. You are not from Gyongyos . . ."

He reached a sudden decision and leaned over to press a button on the instrument console near his chair. Brion was aware of a sudden jab of pain in his forearm and jerked it upwards. Too late. The gleaming needle sank back into the arm of his chair, its work done. He tried to stand, then realized that he could not. Nor could he keep his eyes open. He plunged into blackness . . .

For the first day, Lea had not minded waiting alone in the forest. It was a joy to rest after the ceaseless walking, a profound pleasure to just sit on the bank of the stream and cool her feet in the running water. Through the tall trees she could see the drifting white clouds and the occasional flock of flying lizards calling out as they went by. The rations were as tasteless as ever, but they were filling and took care of her appetite. As the sun set the air cooled down, so she shook out her sleeping bag and slipped into it. Placing the gun by her head as Brion had instructed her. She was worried about him, but she tried not to think about it. The trees made dark patches against the star-lit sky above. Her eyes closed and she drifted off to sleep.

Some time during the night an animal called out hoarsely in the forest and she woke up, startled, reaching for the gun. She had heard these same cries often enough before after dark, but they had not bothered her. Because Brion had been there. His silent bulk had given her the security to go back to sleep, knowing that she could rely on his protection at all times. Only he wasn't with her any more. She had trouble getting back to sleep after that—and woke up more than once to listen to the alien sounds in the darkness. It was a disturbed night from then on, and she did not rest easy until after dawn.

Lea kept busy for most of the next day by going over and revising the record. The computer in the ship played it back to her and she added to it and modified it, bringing it up to date. And tried not to think of Brion going up that narrow canyon, alone. Forced away all thought of what would happen if he encountered any of the tanks.

The second night passed as badly as the first, and dawn found her bleary with fatigue. She washed in the cold mountain stream, then used the comb to do what little was possible with her hair. The dried rations were just as bad as ever, and she was just washing them down with some of the water when she saw the flicker of motion among the trees. There was something there!

She had promised Brion that she would follow his instructions and she did so at once. Seizing up the pistol and sending a hail of explosive slugs into the forest. When she had stopped firing a voice called out to her in Esp⁻ranto.

"We are friends . . ."

More bullets followed the first. She had no friends here! Dropping behind the barrier of stones she watched for movements among the trees. Something coughed mechanically deep in the forest and there was a sudden explosion behind her—then another. Clouds of pungent smoke billowed out, washing over her. She held her breath, but then had to breathe. Coughed, sat down, coughing, lay over on her side with her eyes closed, still coughing. She was silent and unmoving when the masked men filed out of the forest, to stand and look down at her body.

EIGHTEEN

Into The Military Mind

Brion blinked his eyes open and stared up at the unfamiliar ceiling. His thoughts were foggy and it took him some time to remember what had happened. The valley . . . no . . . he had reached the end of the valley . . . the black metal column. Then the soldiers, his capture, an interview with a man named Hegedus. Something happened . . . he remembered now, the injection, a drug, and after that . . . nothing. Except for the sensation that some period of time had passed. He looked down and saw that he was lying on a couch of some kind, placed against the wall of a large and windowless room. The room was furnished with a table and some unadorned metal furniture, chairs that were covered in the same fabric as the couch. Turning his head had made him feel dizzy, and when he sat up he found that he was even more light-headed and had to hold tight to the couch until the sensation went

away. Quick anger replaced the feeling of nausea.
He really did not enjoy being treated in this manner.
And the mystery of Selm-II was just as deep as it
ever had been. He stood, ignoring the dizziness this
time, and walked over to the door and tried the
handle. Locked. He was just turning away when he
heard a buzz from some mechanism inside the door.
The handle turned and the door slowly opened.

Brion stepped to one side and raised his massive
fist. They had captured him once, then drugged him.
They would find that this was not as easy to do a
second time. He owed them something and knew
just what it was. He tensed his muscles as the door
swung wide. Ready!

It was Lea who walked in.

His arm dropped slowly to his side as she turned
towards him. "Are you all right?" she asked. "They
wouldn't tell me."

"How did you get here? Did you follow me?"

"No, I stayed at the site. But I was captured by
soldiers, two days after you left. They came up
quietly and called to me. I remembered what you
had said so I fired at them, even when I couldn't see
them. There were explosions around me, shells of
some kind I imagine, and clouds of smoke. I tried to
get away, but there must have been gas of some
kind in the smoke. I remember falling, and that's all
until I woke up here a little while ago. A woman
came in, she didn't say anything, just led me here.
Except I don't know where *here* is or what is happening?" There was an edge of hysteria to her voice
now and he could see that she was wringing her
hands tightly together. He stepped forward and took
them in his.

"It's all right now. I know little more than you do, but not much. I followed the valley until it ended in a box canyon, a dead end. Then men and soldiers appeared, seized me the same as they did you, and I woke up in this room. I don't think they mean us injury, they would have had all the time they need for that. But who are they—and how did they find you? We need some answers . . ."

"And you shall have them," Hegedus said, coming through the open door. "Dr. Morees, will you please be seated. You too, Brion . . ."

"How do you know my name?" Lea asked.

"Your associate here told us. We have very advanced techniques, drugs and machines, that can extract a person's memories. It is done harmlessly and there are no aftereffects. We learned from Brion about your mission, and where you were waiting for him, so we went to get you before you suffered any more discomforts on that wild world. I'm sorry about the gas, but we knew that you were armed and on your guard. And we also know all about the fine work you are both doing for the Cultural Relationships Foundation. We deeply regret that you have had such difficulties, and our only desire now is to make amends."

"You can start right now by telling us what is happening on Selm-II," Brion said.

"I shall be more than happy to. That is why I am here with you now. Sit down, please. Is there anything you might like? Something to eat or drink . . ."

"Nothing. Except that explanation." Brion's patience was exhausted and he snapped the words. Lea nodded assent.

Hegedus sat down across from them and steepled

his fingers on his crossed knees. "To explain exactly what has happened I am afraid that I must tell you a brief history of this world, the planet named Arao . . ."

"Then—we are no longer on Selm-II?" Lea asked, slightly dazed. Hegedus shook his head.

"You are thousands of light years away, on a planet orbiting a totally different sun. Arao. Our historical research has revealed that this planet was one of the very last to be settled before the Breakdown of the Earth Empire. In fact it was settled by refugees fleeing from the wars that were beginning to flare up right across the known galaxy. My ancestors wished to live in peace and the only way they saw to accomplish this was through heroic struggle, through stealth, hard work and immense sacrifice . . ."

"Would you mind getting the story a little bit closer to the present day," Lea interrupted. "We've all seen a bit of struggle and sacrifice."

"Of course! I apologize. But the background is necessary. Please bear with me a moment or two longer. As I said, two interstellar spacers were obtained, the survivors boarded them and ships headed out into deep space, their course unknown except to a very few. A planet had been discovered, fertile and uninhabited—and far beyond the outermost reaches of the colonized galaxy. Thus they came to Arao, and every year we of the Opole honor Settlement Day with ceremony . . ." He caught the glare in Lea' eye and hurried on.

"But less than a century after we had settled here, on the more verdant of the two great continents this planet is blessed with, sudden tragedy struck. A fleet of great warships descended upon us, remnants of a space armada that had been crushed in battle. They were doing as we did, fleeing the Breakdown. At first there was conflict and death, many perished and the destruction was terrible to behold. But although they had the stronger weapons we had the greater numbers. In the end wisdom prevailed and peace was finally made before mutual destruction seized us both. The invaders agreed to settle on Gyongyos, the other continent, half a world away from us. They did so, and have remained there ever since.

"We now approach the present day. Despite the fact that we shared this world, living in relative peace, the tension was always present. We, as the original settlers, felt that our world had been invaded, had been ravished, and that some day the Gyongyos would invade again and finish us forever. I find that I have no sympathy for Gyongyosian policy, but it can be understood that they had a point of sorts when they continued to arm against us. After all, they were fewer in number and must have felt a certain guilt about what they had done. In any case, this is all ancient history and we now arrive at the present day . . ."

"About time," Brion growled.

"Patience, please. You see around you the pleasant planet of Arao, fertile and benign. In the warm sea are two great continents, filled with the happy descendents of those two groups of settlers. All this would be paradise indeed were it not for the historical events I have just briefly outlined to you. Because of them the military budgets of the two nations are truly tremendous, with arms our leading manufacture, armies our largest social grouping. War, and the threat of war, have always been omnipresent in our thoughts. And we might have gone to war, destroyed this paradise, had it not been for the invention of the Delta Mass Transporter. Our Opole scientists were of course the ones who developed it, but Gyongyos spies soon made it theirs as well. It was the DMT that was our salvation, for it removed the awesome threat of war and planetary destruction from our people."

"By exporting it to *other* people!" Brion said. "I'm beginning to see where this is all leading."

"How very intelligent of you—though it is beginning to be obvious. The DMT is a variation of the FTL, the faster than light drive that powers all interstellar ships. The star ships make their long jumps through FTL space. We do the same thing with DMT—"

"But you don't need a spacer to do it—just a receiver, a beacon to zero in on!" Brion slammed his fist into his open palm. "That metal pole—it's a Delta Beacon. Planted there by your people. Once a ship has gone to a distant planet and left one of those things you can do away with the spaceships altogether."

"Precisely. The plan was a magnificent one. Search ships went out seeking a suitable planet, going on and on until they found Selm-II, the ideal location for war. Great grass pampas for tank operation. The only native life forms simple saurians that our battle computers are set to avoid. Uninhabited by humans . . ."

"Your people were wrong," Lea said. "There *are* people on the planet!"

Hegedus shrugged. "A small mistake . . . "

"For you perhaps. Not for the poor bastards being slaughtered in the middle of your useless war." Brion turned to Lea in sudden realization. "That destroyed mine that we found, the one the locals thought was so holy. It makes sense now. When these military morons launched their war machines there must have been a mining settlement there. In their hurry to start blowing each other up these people never noticed the mine. So their bombers came over and destroyed it. The survivors had to learn to live with this imported war—and they managed to do just that. Survive. Theirs is a dead-end, concentration-camp culture, but it works. No fire because it would draw the attention of the robots. No metal or it will be detected. No permanent settlements that might be seen and attacked. It all makes a terrible kind of sense—now that we know what really happened there." He turned to Hegedus. "You people have a lot to answer for."

Hegedus nodded. "We realize that. After searching your memory we discovered the true situation on Selm-II. We are of course sorry what we did to the local inhabitants. We cannot turn the clock back; what is done is done. However we can give them a peaceful future. The deactivation call has already gone out. The war is over. The aircraft have landed and switched their engines off. Nothing will move again, no bombs will be dropped, no guns will be fired . . . "

"Very nice for you," Lea said. "But what about the hopeless survivors on the planet? Are you just going to leave them in that nasty dead-end culture that you have forced upon them?"

"Of course. We might have taken steps to help

them were it not for the presence of your Cultural Relationships Foundation. Your organization is immensely rich, and designed specifically for this sort of operation. I am sure that the natives will benefit immensely from your presence."

"Have you benefited as well?" Brion asked. "Do you realize now how wasteful and economically insane this endless war has been for your world?"

"You will watch your words!" Hegedus said, angry, losing his composure for the first time. "You sound dangerously like a member of the World Party. Production for consumption not war, more consumer goods, legal unions . . . we've heard it all before. Perverted rot. Anyone who speaks that way is an enemy of society and must be extirpated. The World Party is illegal, its membership confined in labor camps. Armies are freedom, military weakness a crime . . ." He paused, panting, a fine dotting of sweat beading his forehead.

"My, my," Lea said, smiling sweetly. "But we seem to have touched you at a sore spot. After umpteen hundreds of years, it looks as though people are beginning to get tired of military stupidity . . ."

"You will be silent!" Hegedus ordered, jumping to his feet. "You are under military jurisdiction right now. You may be offworlders—but speaking treason is still a punishable crime. What you have said up to now will be ignored. But you have now been warned. Any future remarks will be punished. Do you understand?"

"We understand," Brion said calmly. "In the future we will keep our thoughts to ourselves. Please accept our apology. It was ignorance, not malice, I assure you."

Lea started to protest—then realized what Brion

was doing and stayed silent. Words were not going to stop these martial madmen. They actually lived in a military and jingoist idea of heaven. Wave the flag, my country right or wrong, build up the armament industries, repeal all civil rights—and go to war forever! The generals ruled and they were never going to voluntarily step down from the seat of power. With this realization came the understanding as well that they both were prisoners here. Antagonizing their captors would be the equivalent of committing suicide. Brion's words echoed her thoughts.

"Since you are winding down the war on Selm-II, you must have plans to continue the conflict somewhere else."

Hegedus nodded, taking a kerchief from his side pocket and patting his head with it. "Another planet has been selected from the records of the original searchers. Conferences are now taking place at the highest level in both countries, and arrangements are being made to transfer the operation there."

"Then we are no longer needed here," Brion said, climbing to his feet. "I assume that we can return to Selm-II now."

Hegedus looked at him coldly, then shook his head.

"You will remain where you are. Your case is under consideration of the military authorities now."

NINETEEN

End of a Mission

"What jurisdiction do your military authorities have over us?" Brion said.

Hegedus's composure had returned. "Come, Brion, I explained that fully not a few minutes ago. This country is at war. Martial law prevails. You were found in a war zone, tampering with a vital piece of military equipment. Be happy that we are a civilized people and did not have you shot on the spot."

"And what is your reason for holding me?" Lea asked. "Your thugs dropped grenades on me, then kidnapped me. Is that what 'civilized people' do?"

"Yes. When you are on a spying mission in a war zone. But, please, let us not quarrel. Consider yourselves our guests for the time being. Privileged guests, for you are the first offworlders to ever have set foot upon our planet. Though we have our political differences, Gyongyos and Opole are in complete

agreement about one thing. There is a complete ban
on offworld contact. We both sought refuge here
from the wars of the Breakdown. The rest of the
inhabited galaxy has nothing to offer us."

"The wars have been over for a thousand years,"
Brion said. "Aren't you being a little paranoid?"

"Not in the slightest. We are complete unto ourselves here. We need nothing from the outside. But
outside influence might bring pressures, insidious
political movements that might destroy our happy
way of life. It is a gamble that we can only lose.
Therefore we maintain a strict no-contact policy.
Now, if you will excuse me. Sergeant."

The door opened the instant he had spoken the
words and the Sergeant came in, stamping his
heavy boots as he came to attention. Brion recognized that stern, military face. He was the same man
who had led the squad that captured him. Hegedus
went to the door.

"The Sergeant will stay with you until I return.
Ask him for anything you might need. You should be
getting hungry by now."

Brion was scarcely aware that Hegedus had left,
for the mention of hunger had brought the sudden
realization to him that he was famished. He felt as
though it had been weeks since last he ate. Hunger
had been forgotten in the rush of events—but it
sprang upon him now like a ravenous animal: his
stomach growled loudly.

"Sergeant—can you get us some food?"

"Yes, sir. What would you like?"

"Do you have steaks on this planet?"

"We're not uncivilized—of course we do. And beer
as well . . ."

"For two if you don't mind," Lea said. "Rare. I want to forget completely about dehydrated protein rations for as long as I can."

The Sergeant nodded and spoke a quick order into his helmet microphone. Brion felt his gastric juices surging against his stomach wall. The few minutes that passed before the meal arrived seemed like hours. A soldier came in with the large tray, set it on the table and left. They attacked the food.

"Best steak I have ever had," Brion mumbled around a giant mouthful.

"Not to mention the best beer," Lea said, sighing as she lowered the frosted glass. "You people ought to run tours to this place from the vegetarian planets. Show them what good food is like."

"Yes, mam," the Sergeant replied, eyes firmly front, his jaw set and stern.

"Why don't you join us in a beer?" Brion said.

"Not on duty." Voice toneless, eyes never moving from the far wall.

"What did you do before you went into the army, Sergeant?" Lea asked, nibbling delicately on her food now that the first rush of hunger had been removed. Brion looked at her out of the corners of his eyes and nodded slightly.

"Always been in the army."

"And the rest of your family? In the army too—or perhaps working in factories . . ." The question seemed harmless enough; but the Sergeant knew better. He moved his eyes just enough to glower down at Lea, then looked back to the wall.

"No discussions while on duty."

End of conversation. But Lea would not be put off. "All right, no discussions. But can you tell us about the war? Do you supervise it or watch it or any-thing?"

"Military secret, not to be discussed. But everyone on Arao watches the war. On television every day, all day, very popular too. People bet on different results. Very exciting for everyone."

"I'm sure that it is," Brion said. What was it he had read in a history book once about bread and circuses? "I don't wish to pry, and of course you won't answer if it is a military secret. But do both countries on this planet use the same DMT facility to reach Selm-II? The one where you picked me up."

The Sergeant gave him a cold penetrating look while he made his mind up. "No military secret there. Same facility used by both. Accurate check made that way to see that disarmament is equilat-eral at all times."

"Then what is there to stop one side—the enemy of course—from lying in wait outside to ambush your forces as they emerge?"

"Milneutzone, sir. Known about by everyone who watches television. Coded radio broadcasts prevent any weapons of war from being used within a thirty mile radius of the Delta Beacon. A military neutral-ized zone."

"That explains it," Brion said. "Coming up the valley towards the beacon I confronted a tank with a broken tread. Otherwise it was fully operational. It aimed its guns at me—but never fired. Is that your milneutzone?"

"Probably, sir. Guns won't fire inside thirty miles."

"Did you ever wish that war would end so you . . ."

"No more questions!" The Sergeant barked the words loudly and harshly. The conversation was obviously at an end. They finished the meal in silence. Had just finished when Hegedus returned. The Sergeant snapped to attention, turned and left.

"I sincerely hope that you enjoyed your food . . ."

"That's enough!" Brion's voice was as rough as the Sergeant's. "No politeness. Just tell us what happened."

Hegedus extended this little moment of torture by crossing the room and sitting down before he spoke. After first crossing his legs and smoothing a crease from his trousers.

"I am the bearer of very good tidings. Although you have caused us immense amounts of trouble and disturbance, we are not an unjust people. We do not believe in killing the messenger who brings the bad news. It has been decided to return you at once to Selm-II. All of your equipment will be returned to you upon your arrival there and a staff car will take you to the plain where you can send for your ship. This will be the only machine of ours operating, so you need not be afraid. As soon as you leave it, it will become immobilized as well. The Delta Beacon will also be destroyed as you pass through. All contact with Selm-II will end. Forever."

"You are letting us go—just like that?" Lea seemed shocked—this was the last thing she had expected.

"Why not? I said that we were humane. You were only doing your duty as you saw it—as we do ours. You intended us no injury, nor will you be able to do us any injury in the future."

"What if we do? What if we tell the galaxy about you, so people can come here . . ."

Hegedus smiled coldly while Brion shook his head in a solemn *no*. "It won't be that easy—or even possible. There are millions, probably billions, of stars in this lenticular galaxy. How can we ever find this solar system? We haven't a clue—we have never even seen the sun so we have no idea of even what type it is. Or in what direction it lies. We're out of luck. When the delta beacon goes, so goes all contact with Arao. Forever. Unless they want to contact us."

"No chance in the slightest of that," Hegedus said. "And what you say is perfectly true. We do not want your interference, nor will we ever have it. Officially I have forgotten your subversive Party Statements—but personally I know how you feel. Your quasi-beneficient Cultural Relationships Foundation won't be sneaking in here to change our happy way of life. To stir up the workers and create dissention. We *like* the way we are. You are not going to change anything. We will go now. The less you know about us the happier we will be. Sergeant!"

"Sir!" the Sergeant said, throwing open the door the instant the command had been given.

"Have your squad take these two to the transmission area at once. They are to talk to no one on the way."

"As you command, sir!"

There were eight men in the squad, heavily armed and fully equipped. They entered the room with much stamping and clattering of equipment. With guns at the ready, they formed up in obedience to the Sergeant's shouted orders. Lea had been holding her temper, but all this stamping and shouting and military nonsense was too much for her.

"Murderous madness! You people are the most stupid—"

"Silence!" the Sergeant bellowed, shoving her towards the door. Aiming his drawn pistol at Brion's instinctive motion towards him. "Follow orders and you won't be hurt. Forward . . . march."

There was absolutely nothing they could do. Brion held Lea's arm, felt it shaking, and knew it was rage not fear. He felt the same way. Frustrated. He was willing to try anything—but nothing he did would affect the outcome. They were going back to Selm-II. Alive or dead. And the insanity and waste of this war would continue as long as the planet had resources left to plunder.

They marched down the long metal corridor, footsteps thudding in step. Four soldiers before them, four to the rear. And the Sergeant, a menacing guardian, just a pace behind them.

"If there were only something we could do," Lea said.

"There's nothing. You can't worry yourself over it. We've done our best. The war is over on Selm-II, the people there will be taken care of."

"But what about the people on *this* planet? Are their lives to be stunted and deprived by this useless war . . ."

"No talking," the Sergeant shouted, so close behind them that his voice hurt their ears. "I'll do the talking here. Eyes front. Keep walking."

And then he spoke again, in a whisper so quiet they could just make it out above the sound of the marching boots.

"We're not all like Hegedus, you know. He's a general. He didn't tell you that. We have over six thousand generals in the army. Make more money than a sergeant does, let me tell you. Don't turn around or we're done for! That room was well bugged. I heard everything said. No bugs in this hall. Only a few moments left. People like me, its the army or the factories. Work a nine day week in the factories. No meat, ever. That was a general's steak you had. It's got to end. Maybe you people can help. Tell everyone about us. Tell them we need help. Bad."

There was a large door at the end of the corridor, guarded by two soldiers. The door opened as they approached.

"This is it," the whispered voice said. "You, Brion Brandd, turn around and say something before we reach the door. I'll push you. Have your hand over your chest . . . now!"

Brion took one step, then another. Did the man mean it? Or was this a sadistic trap set by Hegedus? They were almost at the door. It might simply be a plan to kill them both . . .

"Do it!" Lea hissed. "Or, damn you, I will!"

"You can't make us leave like this," Brion shouted, turning on his heel.

"Just shut your mouth!" The Sergeant shouted angrily, slamming his hand into Brion's chest so hard that he was pushed backwards, falling. "Pick him up! Drag him in! The woman too!"

Rough hands seized them both, hauling them forward through the door and into the large room beyond. Hurling them down onto the scratched metal flooring. The soldiers stepped back, guns pointed as they withdrew.

"Put those on," the Sergeant ordered, as technicians advanced with a pair of the thick black suits.

They were dressed in silence, the suits sealed, the faceplates snapped shut. Then they were alone in the middle of the metal-plated area. Brion raised his hand in farewell when the force hit them . . .

They were standing on hard rock, a warm sun shining down on them. Brion whirled about at the sound of a sudden explosion; the Delta Beacon was just a mass of smoking rubble. He stripped off his suit, then helped Lea with hers.

"What happened?" she said, the instant her head was free of the helmet.

"He gave me this," Brion said, slowly opening his hand. A scrap of folded paper lay on his palm. He opened it slowly and smiled at the row of numbers that had been hastily scribbled there.

"Is that what I think it is?" Lea asked.

"It is. Galactic coordinates. A stellar position relative to the navigational centerpoint. A star, a sun . . ."

"With a planet named Arao in orbit around it! Aren't the Cultural Relationships people going to have a fine time designing a social structure that is a little more responsible to the people than the present one."

"Anything would be an improvement. I want to volunteer for this assignment. This is one I am going to enjoy!"

"Say *we*. It may be years before it is done, but I promise to be patient. Because at the end of all that waiting I'll be able to see the expression on Hegedus's face when we walk into the room."

The sun hung over the valley, reflecting bright glints from the small tracked vehicle standing there. As they walked over to it the engine started and it vibrated gently, waiting for them to enter.

"The last machine," Brion said as they closed the door and the vehicle started forward.

There was a box on the seat with all of their equipment still intact inside of it. Lea took out the radio and handed it to Brion. "Please call the life-ship. Give it urgent instructions so it will be waiting for us when we get out of this place. I've had enough of this planet—as well as the last one."

When the canyon emerged onto the grassy plain the silver needle of the spacecraft was standing there before them. The robot car stopped—and the engine died away into silence.

After all the centuries of destruction, the war was finally done.

THE END

HARRY HARRISON

☐	48505-0	A Transatlantic Tunnel, Hurrah!	$2.50
☐	48540-9	The Jupiter Plague	$2.95
☐	48565-4	Planet of the Damned	$2.95
☐	48557-3	Planet of No Return	$2.75
☐	48031-8	The QE2 Is Missing	$2.95
☐	48554-9	A Rebel in Time	$3.50

GORDON R. DICKSON

PHILIP JOSÉ FARMER

THE BEST IN SCIENCE FICTION